All Tomorrows

THE MYRIAD SPECIES AND MIXED FORTUNES OF MAN

C. M. Kosemen

BY THE SAME AUTHOR

Speculative biology and palaeontology

All Tomorrows (2006 edition)

All Yesterdays with John Conway and Darren Naish

All Your Yesterdays

Cryptozoologicon with John Conway and Darren Naish

Culture and history in Turkey

Nişanyan House: A Photographic Essay

Osman Hasan and the Tombstone Photographs of the Dönmes

The Bodrum Jewish Cemetery with Siren Bora

The Disappearing City

A Karakaş Speaks

Memories and Stories of Bodrum's Jewish Community

Hatıratlarda Türkiye Yahudileri with Rıfat N. Bali

Memoirs of an Istanbul Psychiatrist with Henri Griladze

Forests of the Afterlife

Art collections

Tangent Worlds

Alternate Life

Decade

Acknowledgements and Dedication

From the outset, *All Tomorrows* depended on a thriving community of fans to spread, grow, and ultimately evolve into the book you hold in your hands today. Few other titles have been as lucky.

My heartfelt thanks go out to my fans and friends who believed in this project. All of your names are listed on the supplementary web page, accessible through the QR code below.

This book is dedicated to you.

C. M. Kosemen, August 2025

This edition first published in 2025

Wilton Square Books
29 Wilton Square
London N1 3DW
www.wiltonsquarebooks.com

First published by the author in 2006

Text design by Ellipsis, Glasgow

A CIP record for this book is available from the British Library

ISBN 9781806770021

Our authorised representative in the EU for product safety is:
Logos Europe, 9 rue Nicolas Poussin, 17000, La Rochelle, France
contact@logoseurope.eu

Lineage Timeline

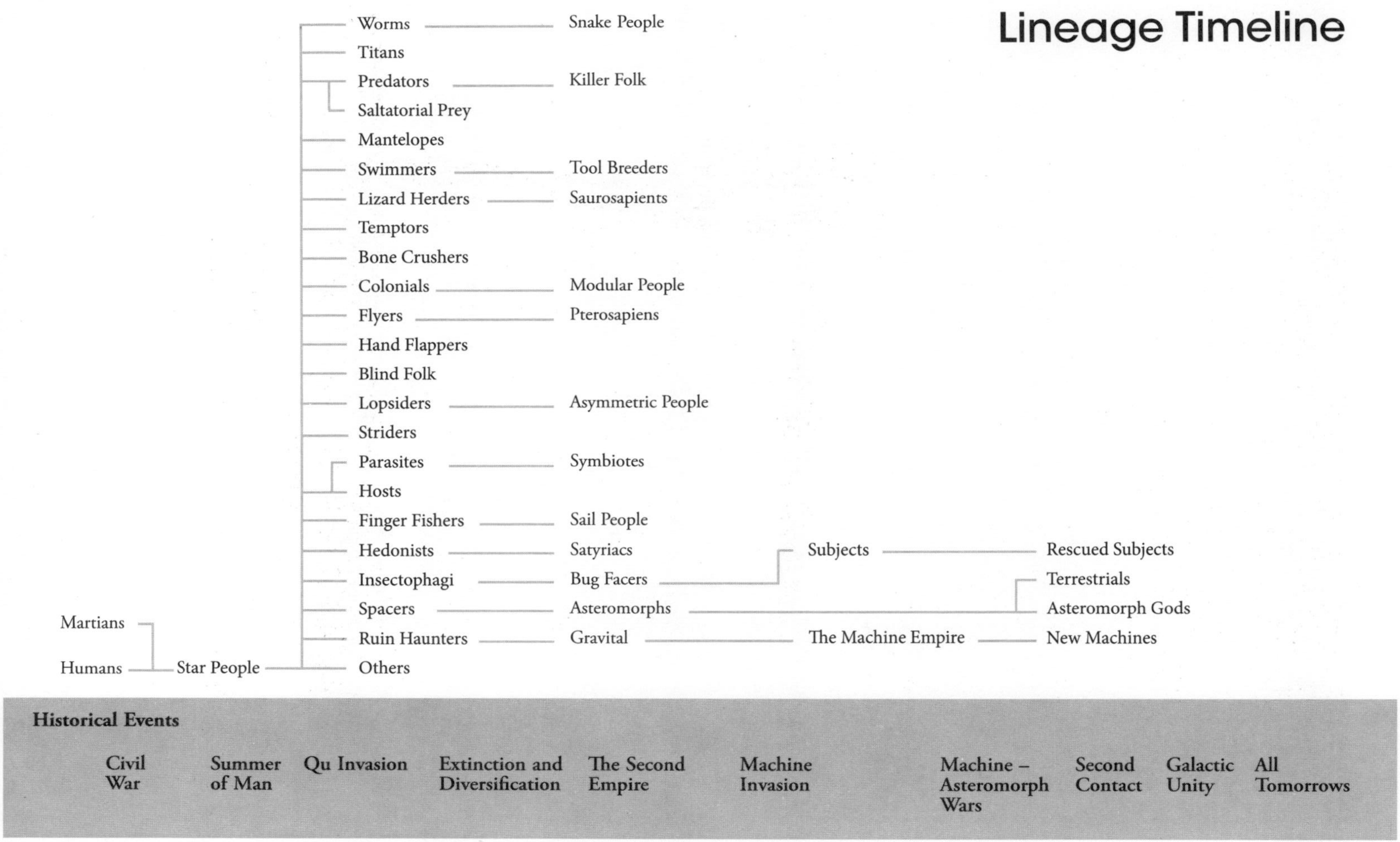

Martians

Humans — Star People

Worms — Snake People

Titans

Predators — Killer Folk

Saltatorial Prey

Mantelopes

Swimmers — Tool Breeders

Lizard Herders — Saurosapients

Temptors

Bone Crushers

Colonials — Modular People

Flyers — Pterosapiens

Hand Flappers

Blind Folk

Lopsiders — Asymmetric People

Striders

Parasites — Symbiotes

Hosts

Finger Fishers — Sail People

Hedonists — Satyriacs

Insectophagi — Bug Facers — Subjects — Rescued Subjects

Spacers — Asteromorphs — Terrestrials

Asteromorph Gods

Ruin Haunters — Gravital — The Machine Empire — New Machines

Others

Historical Events

Civil War

Summer of Man

Qu Invasion

Extinction and Diversification

The Second Empire

Machine Invasion

Machine – Asteromorph Wars

Second Contact

Galactic Unity

All Tomorrows

A lander ferries the first people to the pre-terraformed Eden of Mars.

To Mars

After millennia of terrestrial foreplay, Mankind's noteworthy achievements began with its political unification and the gradual colonisation of Mars. While the technology to colonise this world had existed for some time, the necessary steps were not taken due to political bickering, shifting agendas, and the sheer inertia of comfortable, industrial civilisation.

Only when the risks clearly began to present themselves and Earth's environment began to buckle under the strain of 12 billion industrialised souls did Mankind finally take up the momentous task.

Over the decades, travelling to and later settling on Mars had been envisioned as quick, relatively easy affairs; complicated but feasible and manageable in short term. As push finally came to shove, it became clear that this was not the case.

The process had to go step by step. Atmospheric bombardment with genetically tailored microbes slowly generated a breathable atmosphere in a cycle that took centuries. Later, a few cometary fragments were knocked off-course to bring forth seas, oceans: water. When the wait was finally over, remnants of Earth's flora and fauna were introduced as specially modified Martian remakes.

When everything was ready, *people* came from their crowded world. They came in one-way ships: fusion rockets and atmospheric gliders, packed to the brim with colonists, sleeping in dreams of a new beginning.

The first steps on Mars were taken not by astronauts, but by barefoot children on lush, biosynthetic grass.

Martians

For several hundred years, Mars remained a backwater, prospering but still dim compared with the splendour of Earth, which was glowing brighter than ever before. Thanks to the relocation of environmentally demanding industries to Mars, Earth could import and consume more of everything without having to damage its tired biosphere. It was the Terrestrial Heyday: the climax of economic, cultural and social development on old Earth.

This, however, was not to last. Like the gradual separation of America from its Old World founders, the governments of Mars adopted a new, Martian identity. They declared political independence and called themselves 'Marinerians' – after Mars's Valles Marineris: the largest canyon of the solar system, which after terraforming had become a Mediterranean-like inner sea, uniting different cities and polities on that planet.

The difference between Earth and Mars was not only political. A few generations in less gravity had given the new Marinerians a spindly, lithe frame that would have looked surreal in their old home. This, combined with a certain amount of genetic engineering, took their separation to a new level.

For a while the silent schism between the two planets was mutually accepted, and the balance of power hung in an edgy equilibrium. But the Terra–Martian standoff did not – could not – last for ever. With limitless resources and an energetic population, Mars was bound to take the lead.

Civil War

Martian prominence in the solar system was expected to occur in one of two ways: either through long-term economic gain or by a much shorter but painful armed conflict. For a few centuries, the former method seemed to be working, but it eventually caused a collapse in the most destructive way.

Almost since its establishment, Martian culture was suffused with an explicit theme of rebellion against Earth. Songs, motion pictures and daily publications repeated these notions again and again until they became internalised. Earth was the old, ossified home that held humanity back, while Mars was *new*: dynamic, active and inventive. Mars was *the future*.

This ideology eventually reached its semi-paranoid, revolutionary apex. Roughly a thousand years from now, the nations of Mars banned all non-essential trade with, and travel to, Earth.

For Earth, it was a death sentence. Without the resources and industries of Mars, the Terrestrial Heyday would quickly be over. Since a trade in essential goods continued, nobody would starve. But for every citizen of Earth, the Martian boycott meant the loss of up to three quarters of their annual income.

Earth had no choice but to reclaim its former privileges, by force if necessary. Centuries after her political unification, Terra geared up for war.

Most thinkers (and fantasists) of previous times had imagined interplanetary war as a glorious, fast-paced spectacle of massive spaceships, one-man fighters and last-minute heroics. Nothing could have been further from the truth. War between planets was a slow, nerve-wracking series of precisely timed decisions that spelled destruction on a biblical scale.

Most of the time the combatants never saw each other; most of the time the combatants weren't there at all. War became a duel between complicated, autonomous machines programmed to maximise damage to the other side while trying to last a little longer.

Such a conflict caused horrendous destruction on both sides. Phobos, one of Mars's moons, was shattered and rained down as meteorite hail. Earth received a polar impact that killed off one third of its population. Barely escaping mutual extinction, the peoples of Earth and Mars made peace and reforged a united solar system. It had cost them more than 8 *billion* souls.

Star People

The survivors of the war between Mars and Earth agreed that massive changes were necessary to ensure that such a war never occurred again. These reforms were so comprehensive that they involved not only political and economic changes, but biological changes, too.

One of the greatest differences between the peoples of the two planets was that, over time, they had almost become different species. It was believed that the solar system could never completely unify until this discrepancy was overcome.

The answer was to create a new human subspecies better adapted not only to Earth and to Mars, but also to the conditions of most newly terraformed environments. Their creators endowed these beings with larger brains and heightened talents – greater than the sum of their predecessors, be they Terrans or Martians.

Normally, it would be hard to convince any population to make a choice between mandatory sterilisation and parenting a newfangled race of superior beings. However, memories of the war were still painfully fresh and for the emergency 'Survival Committees' ruling Earth and Mars, such radical measures were easier to enforce and implement. Any resistance to the birth of the new species did not extend beyond muted complaints and trivial strikes.

In only a few generations, the new race began to prove its worth. Organised as a single state and aided by the technological developments of the war, its people rapidly terraformed and colonised Venus, the Asteroids and the moons of Jupiter and Saturn.

Soon, however, even the solar system began to feel constrained. There was scarcely a world, moon, or planetismal devoid of human inhabitation. Even extreme habitats such as Mercury or the dim planetoids of the Oort Cloud were home to research stations and temporary bases. The new people who inherited these sites wanted to go further, to new worlds under distant stars.

Colonisation and the Mechanical Oedipi

Even for the Star People, interplanetary travel was a monumental task. Early minds had boggled over the problem, and fantasies such as travelling faster than light and via hyperspace emerged as the only 'solutions'.

Simply put, it was impossible to take a large number of people with enough supplies to even the closest star to make colonisation feasible. The existing technologies could only slug along at mere percentages of light-speed, making the journey an epoch-spanning affair. Enormous 'generation ships' were conceived and even built, but these succumbed to technical difficulties or on-board anarchy after a few generations.

The solution was first to go there, and *make* the colonists later. To this end, fast and small automated ships were sent forth to the stars. On board were semi-sentient machines programmed to replicate on site and terraform the destination, then 'construct' its inhabitants from the genetic materials stored on board.

A bizarre problem plagued such attempts. The first generation of humans to be manufactured sometimes developed a strange affection for the machines that made them. They rejected their own kind and perished after the massive identity crisis that followed. This technological Oedipus complex was not uncommon; nearly half of all colony-founding attempts were lost through it. Even then, the remaining half were enough to claim the galaxy for the Star People.

Two Star People watch a holographic movie as they lounge under the remnants of their colonised world's indigenous flora. For them, it was a life of continual bliss.

The Summer of Man

Right after Mankind's colonisation of the galaxy came its first true golden age. Reared by machine prophets, the survivors of the Oedipal plagues built civilisations that equalled and even surpassed their forebears on Earth's ancient solar system.

This diffusion across the heavens did not mean a loss of unity. Across the skies, steady flows of electromagnetic communication linked Mankind's worlds with such efficiency that there was no colony that did not know about the goings-on of her distant siblings. The free flow of information meant, among other things, a vastly accelerated pace of technological growth. What could not be figured out in one world was solved by another, and any new developments were quickly made known to all in a realm that spanned centuries of light.

Not surprisingly, living standards rose to previously unimaginable levels. While this did not exactly mean a galactic utopia, it's safe to say that people of the colonised galaxy lived lives in which labour – both menial and mental – was purely optional. Thanks to the richness of the heavens and the toil of machines, each individual had access to more material and greater cultural wealth than some entire nations in humanity's dim past.

While all this development was going on, a curious phenomenon was observed. While alien life was abundant in the stars, no one had encountered any signs of true intelligence. Some attributed this to its overall scarceness, while others went as far as proposing that a divine influence had given preferential treatment to humanity's worlds, resurrecting certain religious fallacies from Earth's distant past.

Putting theories aside, one question still went unanswered. What would actually happen if Mankind ever ran into its equals or superiors in space?

A reconstruction of *Panderavis* shows the creature's rake-like claws, with which it dug furrows in the soil to find food. Opportunistic indigenous animals walk alongside *Panderavis,* looking for morsels left over from its feasting.

An Early Warning

During those times, a small discovery of immense significance warned humanity that it might not be alone.

On a newly colonised world, engineers had stumbled across the fossilised remains of a puzzling creature, considered so because it was vexing evidence that animals from Earth had, somehow, inhabited this alien planet. Justifiably named *Panderavis pandora*, the colossal fossil was that of a bird-like creature with enormous claws. Later research determined it to be a highly derived Therizinosaur, from a lineage of herbivorous dinosaurs that died out millions of years ago on Earth.

While every other large land animal on that colony world had three limbs, a copper-based skeletal system and hydrostatically operated muscles, *Panderavis* was a typical terrestrial vertebrate with calcium-rich bones and four extremities. Finding it on that planet was as unlikely as finding an alien creature in Earth's own strata.

For some, it was irrefutable proof of divine creation. The religious resurgence, fuelled at first by Mankind's apparent loneliness in the heavens, became even more intensified.

Others saw it differently. *Panderavis* had shown humans that entities powerful enough to visit Earth, take animals from there, and adapt them to an alien world were at large in the galaxy. Considering the time gulf of the fossil itself, the mysterious beings would have been millennia older than humanity when they were capable of such feats.

The warning was clear: there was no telling what would happen if Mankind suddenly ran into this civilisation. Benevolent contact was obviously preferred and even expected, but it paid to be prepared.

Silently, humanity once again began to build and stockpile weapons. There were terrible devices, capable of collapsing stars and wrecking entire solar systems. Sadly, in time even these preparations would prove to be ineffectual.

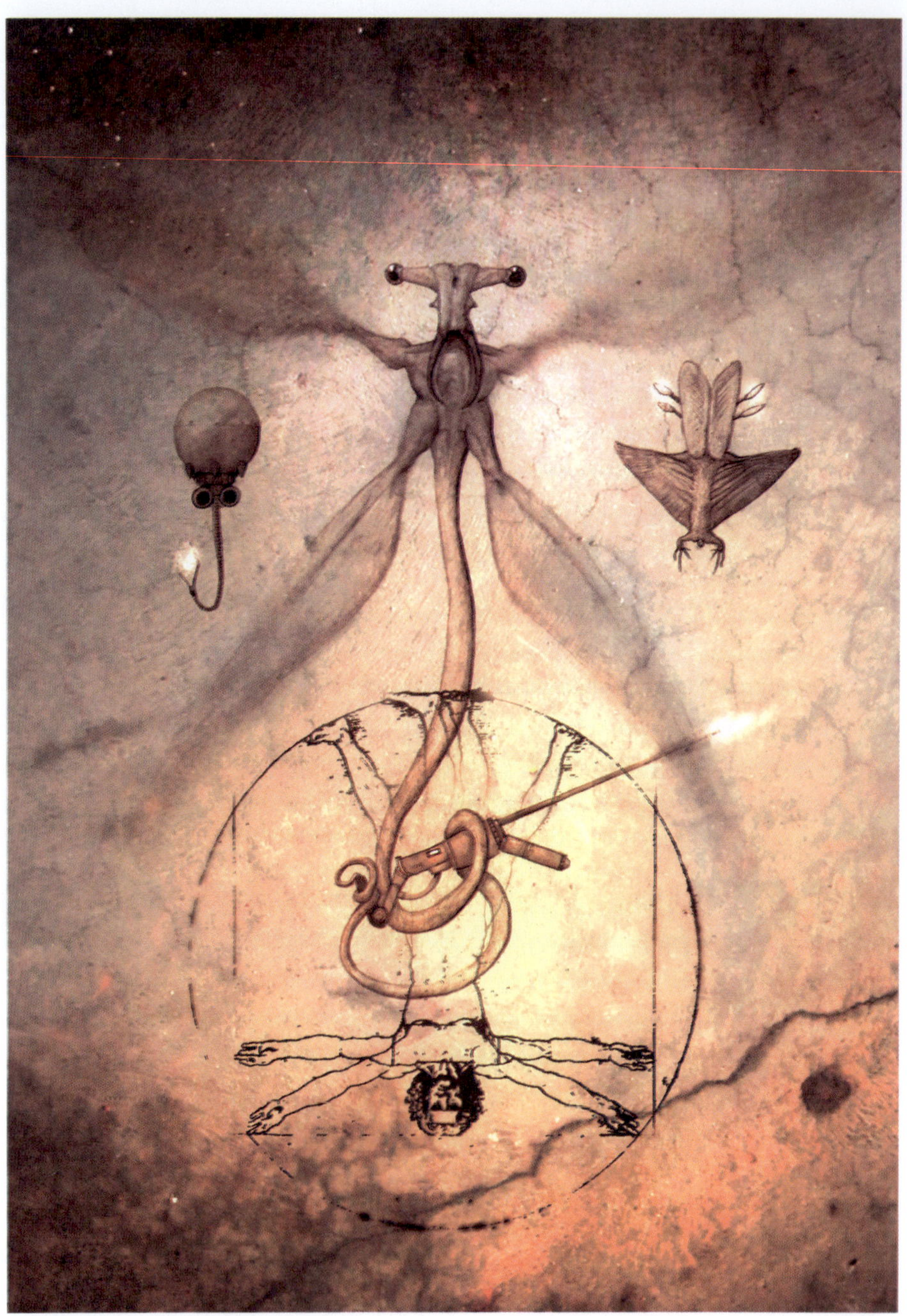

Qu triumphant in the fall of Man. To his left floats a nanotechnological drone; to the right a genetically modified tracing creature.

The Qu

The first contact was bound to happen. The galaxy was simply too large to contain just a single intelligent civilisation. Any delay in contact meant only a heightening of the eventual 'culture shock'. In humanity's case, this culture shock meant the complete extinction of Mankind, as it had come to be known.

Almost a billion years old, the alien species known as the Qu were galactic nomads, travelling from one spiral arm to another in epoch-spanning migrations. During their travels they constantly improved and changed themselves until they became masters of genetic and nanotechnological manipulation. With this ability to control the material world, they assumed a religious, self-imposed mission to 'remake the universe'. Powerful as gods, the Qu saw themselves as the divine harbingers of the future.

This dogma was rooted in what had been a benevolent attempt to protect the species from its own power. However, blind, unquestioning obedience had made monsters of the Qu. To them, humanity, with all of its relative glories, was nothing more than a transmutable subject. Within less than a thousand years, every human world colonised by humans was destroyed, depopulated or, even worse, changed. Despite fervent rearmament, the colonies could achieve nothing against the invaders, save for a few flashes of ephemeral resistance.

Humanity, once the ruler of the stars, was now extinct. Humans, however, were not.

A Qu pyramid towers over a silent world that once housed 4 billion souls. Such structures were the hallmark of the Qu and could be seen on every habitable world they passed through.

Man Extinguished

The worlds of humanity, gardens of terraformed paradise, seemed strangely empty to the Qu. Often there were no raw materials available other than people, their cities and a few basic niches of ecology, populated by genetically modified animals and plants from Earth. This was because humans had first erased the original alien ecologies to begin with.

Outraged by another species trying to remake the universe, the Qu set forth to punish these 'infidels' by using them as the building materials of their own vision. While this led to a complete extinguishment of human sentience, it also saved the species by preserving its genetic heritage in myriad strange new forms.

Surrounded by ersatz humans, now in every guise from wild animals to pets to genetically modified tools, the Qu reigned supreme for 40 million years on the worlds of our galaxy. They erected kilometre-high monuments and changed the surfaces of entire worlds, apparently at whim.

One day, they departed as they had come. For theirs was a never-ending quest and they would not – could not – stop until they had swept through the entire cosmos.

Behind them the Qu left a thousand worlds, each filled with bizarre creatures and ecologies that had once been men. Most of them perished right after their caretakers left, others lasted a little longer to succumb to long-term instabilities. On a precious few worlds, descendants of human beings actually managed to survive.

In them lay the fate of the species, now divided and differentiated beyond recognition.

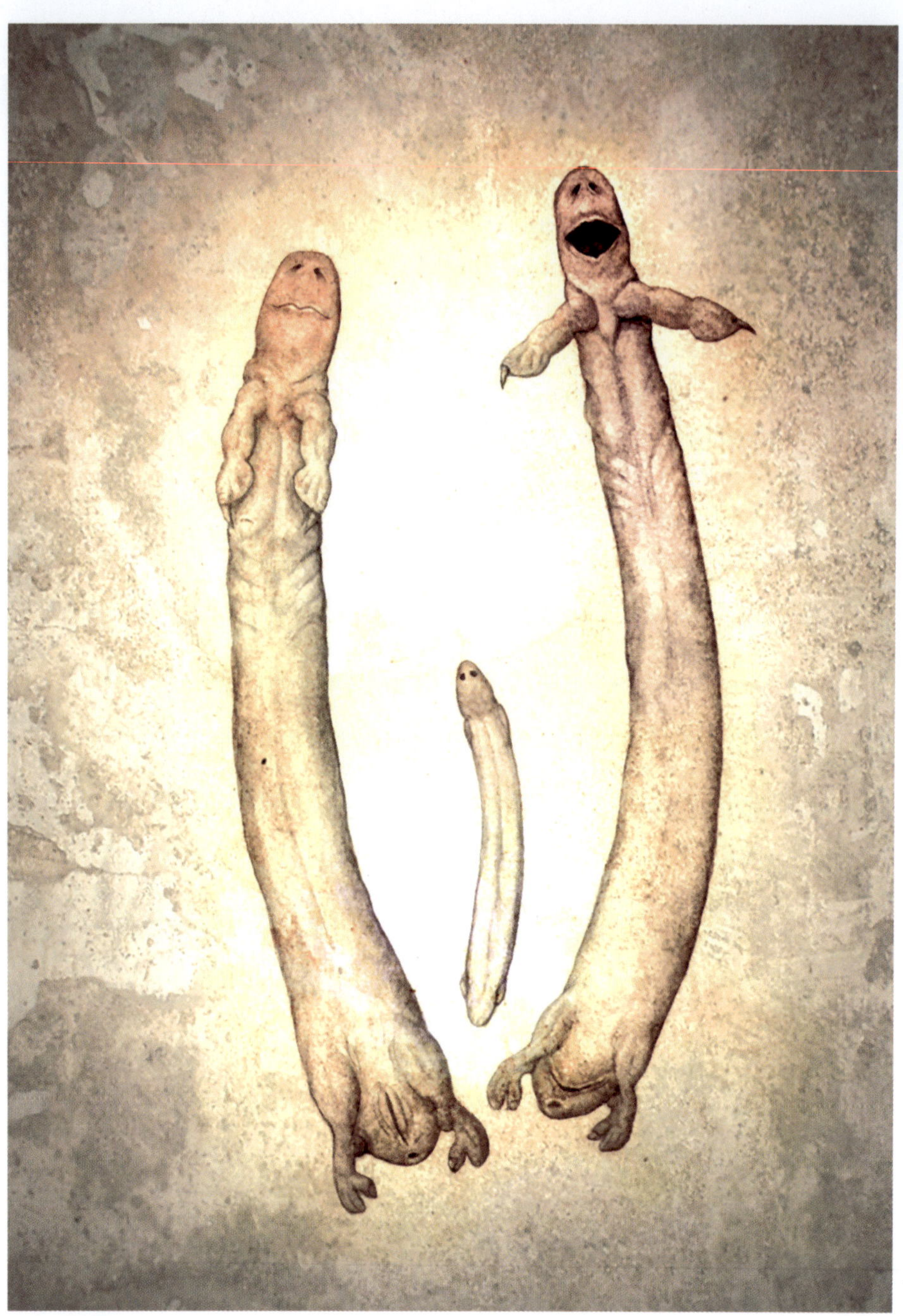

Two Worm parents with their young.

Worms

Their world lay under a scorching sun, its intensity made monstrous through the interventions of the long-gone Qu. The surface lay littered with husks of dead cities, baking endlessly like shattered statues in a derelict oven.

Yet life remained on this unforgiving place. Forests of crystalline 'plants' blanketed the surface, recycling oxygen for the animal life that seethed underground. One such species, barely longer than the arms of their ancestors, was the sole surviving vertebrate. Furthermore, it was this planet's last descendant of the Star People.

Distorted beyond recognition by genetic modification, they looked for all the world like pale, overgrown worms. Tiny, feeble feet and hands modified for digging were all that betrayed their noble heritage. Aside from these organs, all was simplified for life underground. Their eyes were pinpricks and they lacked teeth, external ears and the better half of their nervous system.

The lives of these ersatz people extended little further than continuous digging. If they encountered food, they devoured it. If they encountered others of their kind, they sometimes devoured them too. But mostly they mated and multiplied, and managed to preserve a shred of their humanity in their genes. In time, it would help them prevail.

Titans

On the endless savannah of a long-extinguished colonial outpost, enormous beasts roamed supreme. More than forty metres long by terrestrial measurements, these behemoths were actually the transmuted offspring of the Star People.

Several features betrayed their human ancestry. They still retained stubby thumbs on their elephantine front feet, but these were now useless for any sort of precise manipulation except uprooting trees. They compensated for this loss by developing their lower lip into a muscular, trunk-like organ that echoed the elephants of Earth's past.

As bestial as they seemed, the Titans were among the smartest of the reduced sub-men that remained in the galaxy. Their hulking stance allowed for a developed brain and, gradually, sentience re-emerged. With their lip-trunks they fashioned ornate wood carvings, erected hangar-like dwellings and even began a form of primitive agriculture. With settled life came the inevitable flood of language and literature: myths and legends of the bygone, half-remembered past were told in booming voices across the vast plains.

It was easy to see that, within a few hundred thousand years, humanity could start again with these titanic primitives. Sadly, as a catastrophic ice age descended on the Titans' home-world, the gentle giants disappeared, never to return.

A thumb-claw-sporting predator from one of the devolved worlds most promising for humanity's re-emergence.

A stilt-legged grazing Saltator.

Predators and Prey

Devolved predators were common among humanity's feral worlds. Most of the time they resembled the vampires, werewolves and goblins of bygone lore, hunting equally sub-human prey with a range of derived weaponry. Some had enormous heads with large, lethal teeth. Others tore their victims apart with talon-like feet. But the most common kinds bore modified fingers and thumbs bristling with razor-sharp claws.

The most efficient of these predators lived on what had once been one of Mankind's first interstellar colony worlds. In addition to paw-like hands with switch-blade thumbs they also had gaping, tooth-studded jaws on disproportionately big heads with large, sensitive ears. All of these served to make them the dominant predators on their home planet.

They ran the prairies, stalked the forests and ranged the mountains in pursuit of different people: herbivorous Saltators with bird-like legs. While their prey descended to a completely animalistic level, the hunters managed to keep a spark of intelligence alive in their evolutionary honing.

Mantelopes

Not all post-humans descended into a completely animal existence straight away. Some held on to their minds while losing all of their physiological advantages to the genetic meddling of the Qu.

One species was a prime example. They had been bred as singers and memory-retainers, acting much like living recording devices during the reign of Qu. When their masters left, they barely survived, reverting to a quadrupedal stance and occupying a niche as grazing herd animals. This change was so abrupt that the newly evolved Mantelopes only endured because their artificial biosphere was initially devoid of predators and competing herbivores.

The Mantelopes, equipped with entirely human minds and animal bodies unable to act on the world, lived agonising lives. They could see and understand the world around them, but due to their bodies they could do nothing to change it. For centuries, mournful herds roamed the plains, singing songs of desperation and loss. Entire religions and oral traditions were woven around this crippling disability, as dramatic and detailed as any once found on Earth.

Fortunately, the selective forces of evolution made their agony short-lived. Simply put, there was no advantage to developing a brain if it could not be put to good use. A dim-witted, half-minded Mantelope grew up faster than a smart one, and grazed just as efficiently. The Mantelopes' animal children overtook them in less than a few thousand generations, and their melancholic world fell silent for good. Nothing was sacred in the evolutionary process.

Swimmers

Perhaps because their own life cycle involved an aquatic larval stage, the Qu had transmuted a large number of their human subjects into a bewildering array of aquatic creatures. Taken care of by specially bred attendants, these post-human water babies came in every shape and size imaginable. There were limbless, ribbon-like varieties of eel-people; huge, whale-like behemoths; decorative people who swam by squirting water out of their hypertrophied mouths; and horrifying multitudes of brainless wallowers that served as food stock.

All of them were perfectly domesticated. Most went extinct when their masters left, save for a few lightly mutated, generalised forms. These remaining swimmers still resembled their human ancestors to a large degree: they had no gills, their hands were still visible through their front flippers, their feet were splayed affairs that functioned as a pair of tail flukes. Recognisably human eyes peeked through their blubbery eyelids and they spoke to each other, though not with words and never in sentient understanding.

For millennia they swam the oceans of their ecologically stunted world, feeding on ever-diversifying fish and crustaceans – survivors of the food stock originally imported from Earth. Without the Qu and their intervention, natural selection resumed. The swimmers became more streamlined to better catch their fast prey. The prey responded by getting even faster, or evolving defensive counter-measures such as armour, spikes or poison. Their evolution back on track, the swimmers drifted further and further away from their sentient ancestry. They would wait for a long time indeed to taste that blessing again.

A Lizard Herder scans the world with blank eyes as his stock grow stronger and smarter. The future does not seem to belong to him.

Lizard Herders

They were the lucky ones. Instead of unrecognisably distorting their appearance as they had done to most of their subjects, the Qu had merely erased their sentience and stunted the development of their brains.

Distantly resembling their ancient forebears on Earth, the primitive beings led feral lives for an unnaturally long time. They never regained sentience after the Qu left, despite having every incentive to do so. This was partially due to the total absence of predators on their artificially maintained ecology, resulting in no advantage for intelligence. Furthermore, the Qu had made some small but integral changes to their brains, tweaking with the structure of cerebellum so that certain features associated with heuristic learning could never emerge again. Once again, the reasons for these baffling changes remained known only to the Qu.

The slow-witted people eventually settled into a symbiosis with some of the other creatures that inhabited their planet. They began to instinctively 'farm' some of the large, herbivorous reptiles, ancestors of which were brought from Earth as pets.

Soon the balance of this mutualism began to tip in the reptiles' favour. The tropical climate of the planet gave them an inherent advantage, and they underwent a spectacular radiation of different species. They encountered no competition from the only large mammals on the planet – the brain-neutered descendants of the Star People. Faced with a reptilian takeover, the only adaptation these sub-men could muster was to slip quietly into bestial oblivion.

Male and female Temptors, illustrating the sexual differences characteristic of their species. Note the female's elongated, pit-like vagina. When mating, the males walked into these structures as if they were descending into a cave.

Temptors

In the Temptors' case, the remodelling was done with an almost artistic enthusiasm. How they managed to survive in their bizarre form is not clear; their ancestors were used as sessile decoration and through some miracle of adaptation they had endured.

No human would have recognised the Temptors as their descendants. The females were tall, beaked cones of flesh, rooted in soil like grotesque carnivorous plants. The males, on the other hand, resembled contorted, bipedal, beaked apes. Unlike their mates, they were perfectly ambulatory; dozens of them ran around the females' mounds like so many imps. Some would gather food, others would clean the females, while others still would stand guard against danger.

Although their actions looked purposeful, the males had no will of their own. In Temptor society, females controlled everything. Using a combination of vocal and pheromonal signals, they guided the masculine hordes to any number of menial tasks, while mating with the strongest, the most obedient and the least intelligent to produce even better drones. At certain times they would also give birth to a few precious females, who would be carried away by subservient males to root themselves.

It was an extremely efficient hegemony that would certainly have given rise to civilisation in a matter of centuries had fate not intervened. When a stray comet obliterated the Temptors' mound forests, one of humanity's best chances for re-emergence was cruelly swept away.

Bone Crushers

Through the deliberate modifications of the Qu and the blind moulding of evolution, the former worlds of humanity came to be populated with creatures whose outlandish forms would make the myths and legends of ancient days seem tame by comparison.

Their ancestors were pint-sized pets of the Qu that were bred for the dazzling colours of their tooth-derived beaks. When their masters left, most of these pampered creatures died, with no one and nothing left to take care of them.

But some, belonging to the hardiest breeds, survived. In less than an evolutionary eye-blink of a few million years, the descendants of such creatures radiated into the evolutionary vacuum of their garden world. One lineage led to a profusion of herbivorous forms. These were preyed upon by a variety of enamel-beaked raptors, each evolved to deal with a specific prey. Among these generalised niches were multitudes of specialised animals, resembling anything from ibis-billed swamp-sifters to splendorous forms with bizarre crests that flared out of their toothy beaks.

There were even lineages which had reattained sentience, in the shape of the ogre-like Bone Crushers. To an observer today they would indeed be the stuff of nightmares: hairy, and sporting vicious thumb-claws and enormous beaks that suited their scavenging diet. Despite the coarseness of their mental architecture, these corpse-eating primitives were one of the first species to attain intelligence and build a rudimentary civilisation. All of this might prove the futility of human prejudice in the post-human galaxy: a creature could feed on putrefying meat, stink like a grave and express its affection by defecating on others, yet it could also represent Mankind's best chance for the redevelopment of galactic civilisation.

In the event, however, not even the Bone Crushers fulfilled this promise. Their dependency on carrion for food severely limited their population growth, and their medieval civilisations crumbled after a few uneventful millennia.

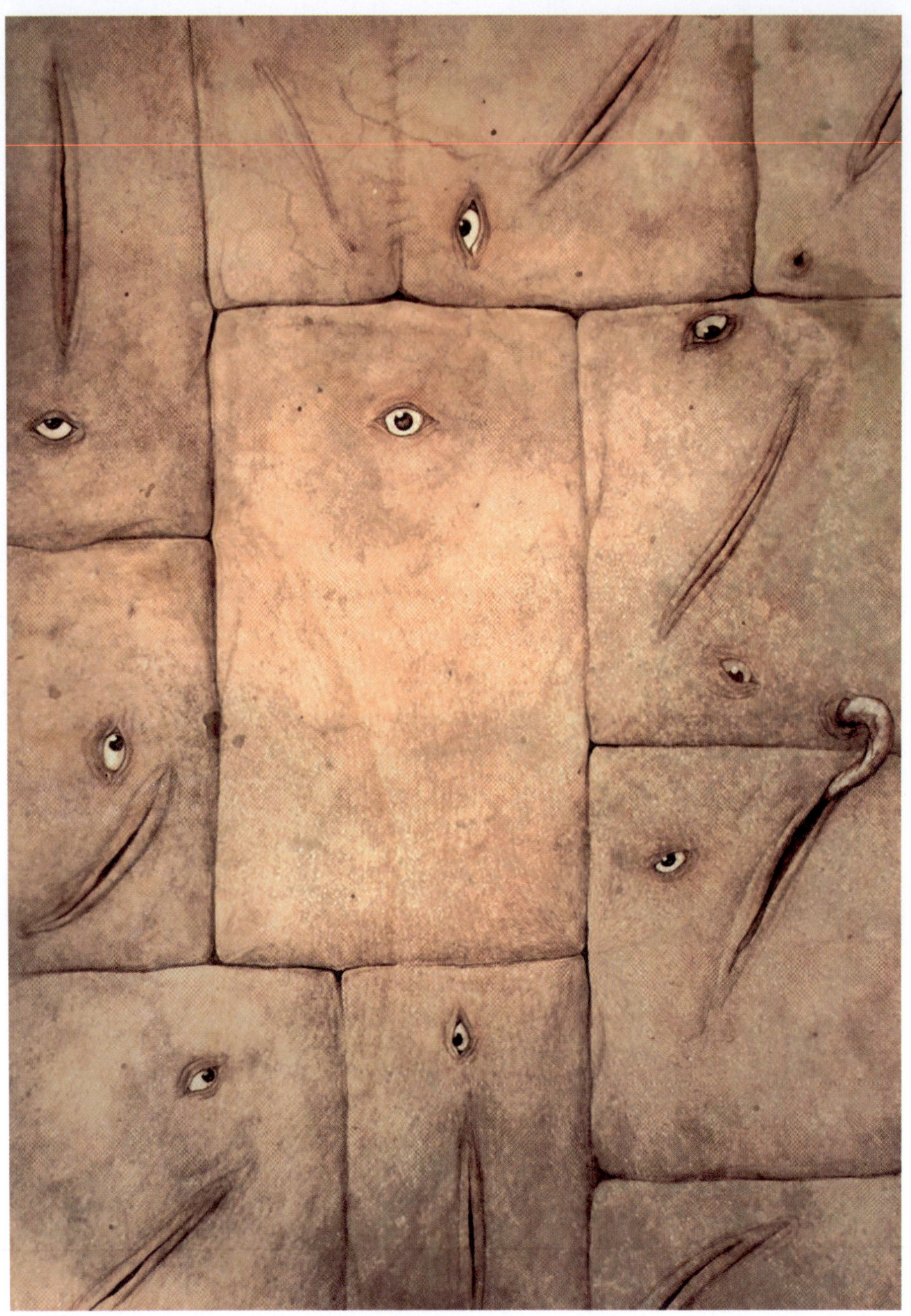

A section from a Colonial field shows the misery that compromised their entire lives. Note that these creatures could reproduce through both asexual budding and more familiar methods.

Colonials

Their world had put up the toughest resistance to the Qu onslaught. So tough, in fact, that they had turned back two successive waves of the invaders, only to succumb to the third.

The Qu, with their twisted sense of justice, wanted to make them pay. Even extinction would be too light a punishment for resisting them. The humans of the rogue world needed a sentence that would remind them of their humiliation for generations to come.

So, they were made into disembodied cultures of skin and muscle, connected by a skimpy network of the most basic nerves. They were employed as living filtering devices, subsisting on the waste products of Qu civilisation like mats of cancer cells – and purely to witness and to suffer more greatly still their wretched fate, their eyes, together with their consciousness, were retained.

Millions of years passed on their world, and they suffered: generation after generation were born into lives of endless misery.

When the Qu left, they hoped for a quick extinction. But their lowliness had also made them efficient survivors. Unchecked by the Qu, the Colonials spread across the planet in quilt-like fields of human flesh. After an eternity of tortured lives, the human fields tasted something that could almost be described as hope.

An ancestral Flyer in her native element. Although ungainly, these creatures had an artificial metabolic advantage that gave them tremendous evolutionary potential.

Flyers

They were not uncommon at all in the dominion of the Qu. Numerous worlds sported human-derived flying species of one kind or another. Most resembled the bats or the pterosaurs of the distant past, dancing through the ether like angels (or demons, depending on the point of view). There were also a few bizarre kinds that relied on swollen gas glands for flotation.

Sadly, most of these creatures were already too specialised to be anything other than flyers. They had lost their potential for reattaining humanity as a result of the extreme adaptations they had developed for powering flight. They had little potential for evolutionary niches beyond this mode of existence.

The only exception proved to be a monkey-like species that flew on wing membranes incorporating the last two fingers. Their advantage was a unique, turbine-like heart, engineered by the Qu during their regime. No other human Flyer in the galaxy had such an adaptation. The starfish-shaped organ sat in the middle of the chest, directly funnelling oxygen from the lungs to the bloodstream in a supremely efficient way. This meant that the Flyers could develop energy-consuming adaptations, such as large brains, without having to give up their power of flight.

They did not evolve into sentient forms right away. Instead, the Flyers exploded into the skies, filling the heavens with anything from bomber-sized sailers to impossibly fast predators that raced with sound. Their world was pristine and there were plenty of niches vacant for them to fill. Intelligence could wait a little longer.

A Hand Flapper on the edge of his mating territory during his comically exaggerated sexual display. Theirs would be a boisterous, ecstatic but ultimately ephemeral existence.

Hand Flappers

Some flying post-humans re-evolved to achieve sentience in an entirely different way. Without the augmented metabolisms or the gravitational advantages enjoyed by their sibling races on distant planets, they had to evolve into flightless forms before they could reattain sentience.

The Hand Flappers were one such species. Their wings, once used for butterfly-like flutters in the unearthly gardens of the Qu, had shrunk and reverted back to their manual condition. Their legs also readapted, but bore a splayed awkwardness from their perching ancestry.

Only a singular and almost sadistically simple flaw held them back from developing civilisation. In the course of their secondary atrophy, the wings of the Hand Flappers had become useless as hands as well. Their flag-like appendages were very useful in signalling and mating dances, but they could not hurl missiles, construct shelter or even manufacture basic stone tools. All they could do with their useless hands was signal their sexual availability, so the Hand Flappers did just that – flashing and dancing their way to oblivion.

A startled Blind Folk father with his one-year-old daughter. Although he knows to stay still in order to confuse sonar-equipped predators, the youngster screams and soils herself in terror. Their attenuated fingers are hallmarks of a lifetime spent in darkness.

Blind Folk

When the Qu came, the Blind Folk dug in, and dug in deep. Inside several continent-sized shelters under their besieged world, they waited for the invaders to pass them by. It was a futile gamble. The Qu located the shelter-caves and remade their inhabitants without effort.

The shelters became home to an entirely different ecology, a realm of perpetual darkness fuelled only by a trickle of water and nutrients from the outside world. A surprisingly complex ecosystem developed from this scant resource; gigantic pale insects, the descendants of common household pests, competed with sightless birds and rodents over fields of overgrown fungi. Predators were not uncommon; crocodilian fish patrolled the underground streams, and vast blind bats, echolocating with unnerving precision, preyed on the residents of the cave floor. The kilometre-high ceilings of the shelters glowed in the dark with protean constellations of bioluminescent fungi and, in some cases, animals.

People were present here as well, albeit in unfamiliar forms. They were more often heard than seen as they tried to find their way in the dark with banshee-like screams. These albino troglodytes lived in a realm where sound and touch, not sight, unlocked the gateway to perception. They had developed long, tactile fingers, enormous whiskers and mobile ears to navigate the dark. Where their eyes should have been, there was nothing but a patch of haunting, flawlessly smooth skin. Their perfect adaptation to the world of darkness had erased the most basic feature of human recognition.

As adapted as they were, they were doomed. Before the Blind Folk could develop any kind of intelligence to crawl out of their artificial habitats, the gradual movement of their world's continental plates snuffed out the shelters one by one.

A Lopsider feeds some indigenous pets native to his high-gravity world. The domestication of native fauna was the Lopsiders' first step on the long journey towards civilisation.

Lopsiders

The Qu were grotesquely creative in their redesign of the human worlds. They transported one group of unfortunate souls to a planet with extreme gravity and redesigned their bodies for life in this bizarrely inhospitable realm.

The results of these experiments resembled nightmarish sketches by Earth's bygone artists: Bosch, Dali or Picasso. Their bodies looked like they had been squashed between sheets of glass. Three out of their four limbs had become paddle-like organs for crawling. Only one of their arms remained, as a spindly tool of manipulation. This singular, wizened limb also doubled as an extra sensor, like the antenna of an insect.

Their faces were different horrors altogether. All pretensions to symmetry – the hallmark of terrestrial animals, from jawless fish onwards – were completely and utterly done away with. One bulging eye stared directly upward while another scanned ahead, in the direction of the creature's vertically opening jaws. The ears were, likewise, distorted.

Monstrous as they looked, these creatures thrived in their heavy-gravity environment. Once again there was the usual explosion of species into every available niche, and the Lopsiders consolidated their chances for renewed sentience.

Striders

While the Lopsiders were designed to live under extreme gravity, another species had been adapted to life by the Qu under the exact opposite conditions – on a gas-giant moon with a fraction of Earth's gravity.

It was a world of wonders, where even the grass grew as tall as trees and the trees were beyond belief, towering to sizes attained only by the skyscrapers of antiquity. In these surreal forests lived equally spectacular fauna – the descendants of the pets, pests and livestock of humans – not to mention the descendants of humans themselves.

One could see them in the spire-like forests, almost dancing among the trees as they reared higher and higher to browse. Their arms, legs and necks had been stretched impossibly thin, while great flaps of skin blossomed throughout their bodies to dispense excess heat. Sometimes they would even change their colour in order to reflect light and keep cool. Overheating was a great problem for their grotesquely tall, lanky bodies.

Although imposing, these attenuated wraiths were so overdeveloped that they had become sickeningly fragile. Even on their gravitationally forgiving world, a fall could shatter their bones and falling from a height could have fatal consequences. Sometimes, on the open plains, even a strong wind could bring them down like toppling masts. They survived entirely due to the merciful conditions of their garden world, but these would soon change drastically.

A few hundred thousand generations after the Qu left their towering works of human art, a lineage of fearsome predators evolved from the terrestrial poultry that had gone feral on the planet. Resembling attenuated versions of their dinosaur ancestors, the predators swept through the garden world like wildfire, extinguishing any species too fragile to escape or resist. The peaceful, delicate Striders were among the first to go.

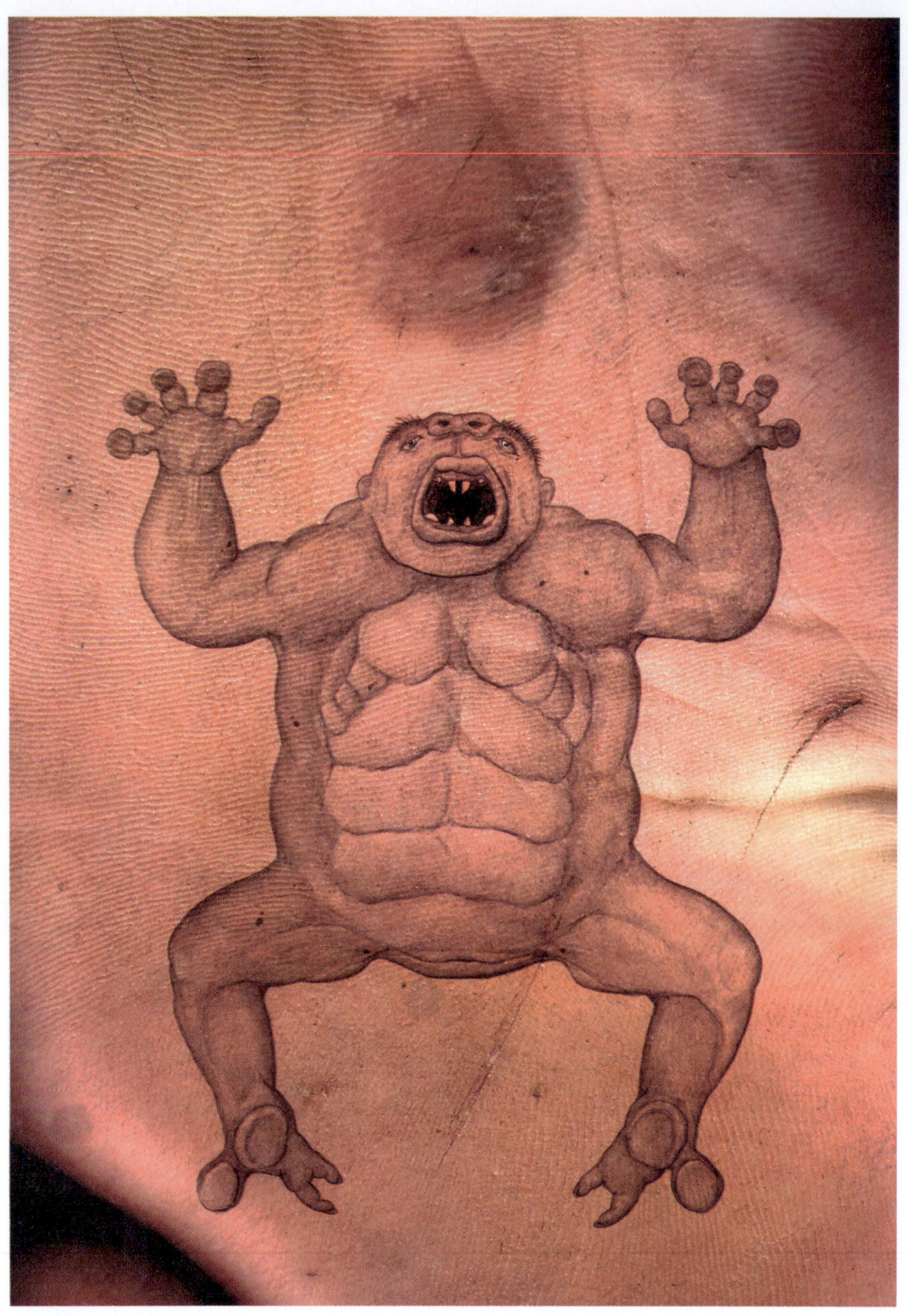

A Parasite shown to scale. Although their fate seems inhumane in every aspect to an observer of today, their very survival shows that such subjective values are irrelevant in matters of long-term survival.

Parasites

Humanity had diverged into two separate lineages on this world. On the one hand, there were several races of almost enfeebled post-humans, similar to their ancestors in outward form, yet mentally equivalent only to animals. They had been degraded by the Qu for managing to turn back their initial wave of invasion. Yet simple atavism was too light a punishment; their twisted relatives, the Parasites, made up the second part of their sentence.

There were actually several kinds of parasitic ex-people, ranging from tortoise-sized ambulatory vampires to the more common, fist-sized variety that lived attached to their hosts. There was even a tiny, endoparasitic kind that infested the wombs of their female victims like ghastly, surviving abortions.

All of these evolutionary tortures were played out under the careful scrutiny of the Qu for millions of generations. The punishment was so baroque, so elaborate that most of the engineered parasite–host relationships died out when the Qu left. Some subhumans learned to cleanse themselves of their tick-like relatives by drowning, burning or even eating them. Others, like the uterine infestors, died out as their aggressive method of parasitism effectively sterilised their hosts.

One or two varieties managed to cling on to their hosts, with abdominal suckers, muscular, gripping limbs or sterile, pain-soothing saliva. But their success did not lie entirely in the strength of their parasitical advantages. They also regulated the numbers of their feeble-minded hosts by not killing them through over-infestation. After all, a perfectly adapted Parasite was one that cared for its host too.

Totally one-sided relationships are rare in any ecology, natural or artificial. Over time, the cousin species' vicious parasitism began to give way to something more beneficial for both sides.

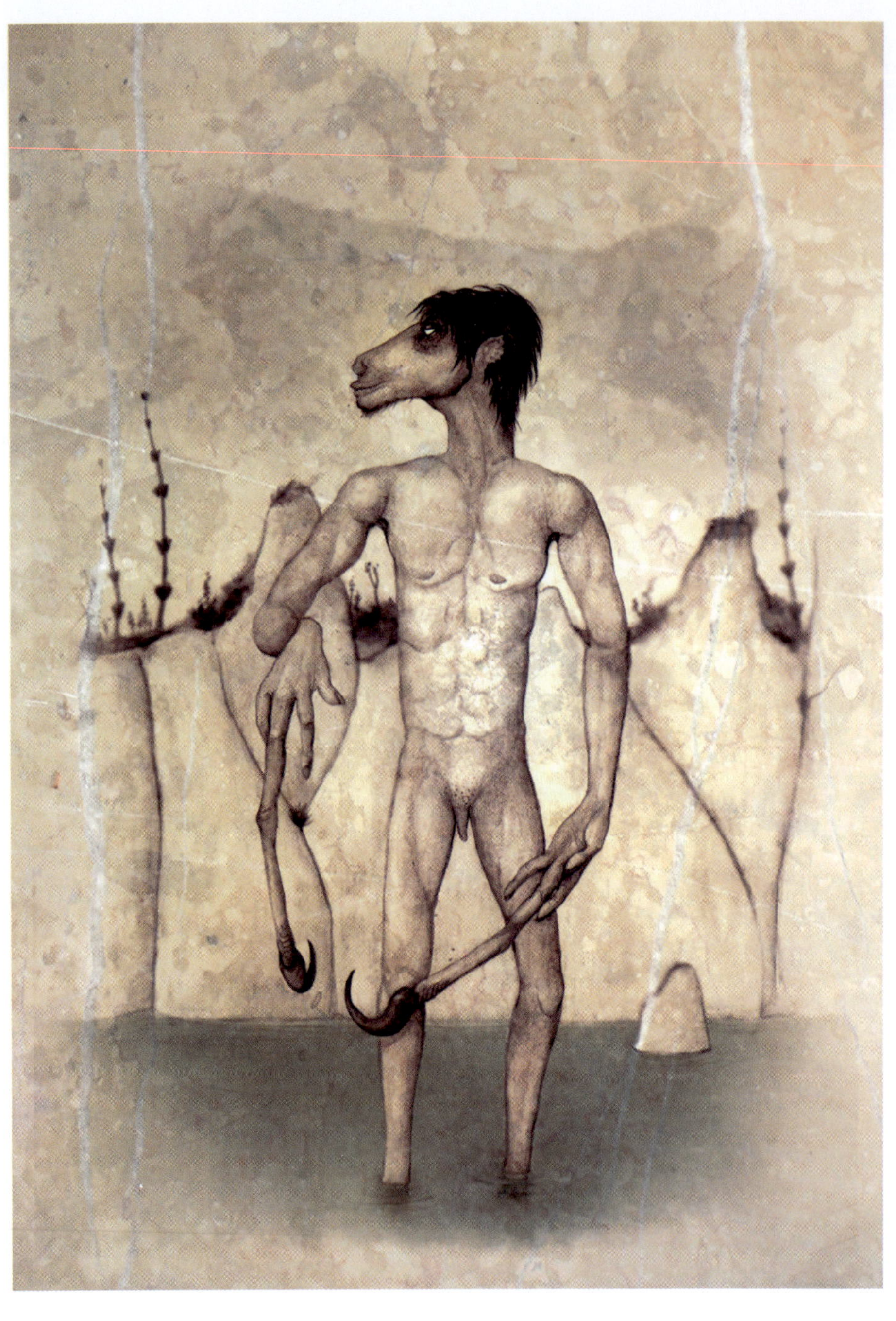

Finger Fishers

Their ancestors had been trapped on an archipelago world – a planet sprinkled with many small continents and countless islands over interconnected networks of calm, shallow seas. Like a magnified Aegean, this place was a terrestrial paradise in many respects. Except that following the Qu, no minds were left to enjoy it.

On this vacant biosphere, evolution was quick to begin her blind, unpredictable dance. Once feral, the descendants of degenerate humans adapted themselves to every available niche, no matter how exotic, how outlandish. One group learned to pluck fish from the lazy shores. Millennia passed and they settled into their piscatorial lifestyle: elongated fingers became moveable fish hooks; teeth modified for a generalised diet became needle-like affairs, lined up neatly in a long, thin muzzle. In less than a hundred thousand generations, the Finger Fishers established themselves as a prominent lineage. There was scarcely a beach, an island or an estuary that was devoid of their pale, lanky form.

As prolific as they were, the Fishers were still no better than animals. Their 'humanity' would come only after another spasm of outlandish adaptations.

Hedonists: the favourites of the Qu. Here a female lies alone on a beach, contemplating absolutely nothing. Without any pressure from the world, their days made themselves as they went along.

Hedonists

Even the blissful existence of the Finger Fishers would have seemed bothersome to the Hedonists – for their kind was not evolved, but *designed* for a life of pleasure. The Qu had kept them as pampered pets, set loose in a tropical island-world of succulent fruits, bountiful trees and calm, lapping lakes full of sweet, bacterial manna. Furthermore, the Hedonists were left as the only animal life on this place. They had no choice but to enjoy it to the fullest.

In normal conditions, any given species would quickly crowd out such a utopian environment. But normal conditions had never been the point of the Qu redesign. They had altered their subjects so that they could conceive only after mating with an enormous number of potential suitors, continually, over a period of decades. Furthermore, reproduction took place through cocoon-like 'casks' buried underground by the females. These unusual, egg-like forms lay dormant for a number of years like plant seeds, and later released fully mature adults into the world. While these extraordinary modifications kept the species at a stable population, it also made them less adaptable. Without any point in sexual competition, natural selection would progress at only a glacial pace. Fortunately, their stable world remained free of environmental catastrophes, even after the Qu left.

All these changes had made the Hedonists' day, too. Their lives consisted of pleasant routines: browsing for food, ecstatic sexual activity, rest and sleep – all while remaining untroubled by concerns of disease or pregnancy. Aloof and carefree, they enjoyed the most pleasurable time of all Mankind, albeit with stunted intellectual capabilities.

It didn't really matter, though. After all, who needed to think when they were having such a nice time?

An Insectophagus and its meal.

Insectophagi

Nondescript, quaint human species abounded in the post-Qu galaxy. Hundreds of them lived out simple, unnoticeable lives, never developing to become sentient, never learning of their origins as human beings who had once ruled the stars. Most of them became extinct, not to be missed or even remembered. Those that lingered on managed to survive in shady, quiet niches, never again making any impact on the celestial scheme of things.

One such species were the Insectophagi. They had become adapted to a diet of colony-building insects and small animals: they had faces covered with protective leathery plates, claw-like hands to dig out prey and worm-like tongues to scoop them up.

All in all, they were not special in any particular way, but a combination of galactic invasions, coincidence and pure luck would later make them among the last surviving descendants of the Star People.

The meek would inherit the cosmos – but not yet. For now, the Insectophagi were concerned only with the locations of insect colonies and the onset of the mating season.

In the aftermath of the Qu invasion, Spacers like this individual will be the only truly sentient human beings to have survived. They were so comfortable in their weightless refuges that the fates of their cousins on other worlds did not concern them. They were also painfully rare; their entire population in the Milky Way galaxy numbered no more than a few dozen arks and a few billion souls.

Spacers

It must be remembered that the Star People did not succumb entirely to the Qu invasion. While their worlds fell away, one by one, some Star People took refuge in the void of space. One after another, entire communities scrambled into generation ships and cast themselves off into the darkness, hoping to go unnoticed by the beings that had overrun their galaxy.

Desperate times made for desperate measures. As the Star People had observed during their initial colonisation of the galaxy, life on generation ships inevitably lead to mass insanity and anarchy. This time, however, humans *had* to adapt themselves – or face extinction.

Entire asteroid fields were confiscated and hollowed out to make spaceships of a size never seen before. The hollow shells cradled bubbles of precious air and water, but no artificial gravity of any kind. It was discovered that a purely ethereal existence would ease the stress of interstellar exile, provided that its inhabitants were adapted for life in such an environment.

Thus, people themselves were forced to change. In an atmospherically sealed, gravity-free environment, their bones were left free to grow longer, thinner, spindlier. The circulatory and digestive systems became pressurised to avoid heart problems and congestion. The latter change had another advantageous side effect: humans could navigate through the void with jets of air expelled from modified anuses.

Such ventures were numerous and usually beset by failure. Yet they did succeed in creating a future. Sealed tight in their moon-sized, air-filled, weightless havens, the descendants of the Star People managed to evade the scourge of the Qu.

It was a never-ending diaspora. Even after the Qu left, the Spacers would find themselves too divergent to have anything to do with their ancestral lifestyles. The survivors of the initial hurdle would never set foot on a planet again.

Only a few hundred generations after the departure of the Qu, a Ruin Haunter wanders among the shattered remains of a city of the Star People. The dominating form of an even greater Qu pyramid can be seen in the background.

Ruin Haunters

One particular human species, singled out for its fortuitous access to the heritage of its stellar ancestors, would eventually play a leading role in the shape of things to come.

The Ruin Haunters had got through the Qu invasion with relatively little degradation; true, they had been reduced to the level of apes, but their recovery had been quick. It seemed the Qu had not worked as hard to suppress their intelligence. Nor had they made an effort to wipe away the material traces of the Star People. Even after millions of years, enormous ruins of the global urban spaces littered the continents of their world. Thus did the Ruin Haunters earn their name.

With developed minds and unrestricted access to the wisdom of the ancient cities, the exponential pace of their development was to be expected. One by one, they deciphered and built upon the secrets of the bygone Star People, until they almost equalled their galactic ancestors in wisdom and skill.

All of this development happened in an unnaturally short span of time, and sometimes the old technologies were not understood even as they were blindly replicated. Needless to say, such a pace of development put premature stresses on the social and political structures of the Ruin Haunters. They barely survived the five world wars that raked their planet, two of which were thermonuclear exchanges.

But they made it through, and their baptism of fire had hardened and awakened them. The wars united them politically and pushed their technological capabilities beyond even the level of the Star People. Coincidentally, they also developed a dangerous form of autochthonous madness; the Ruin Haunters had come to believe that they were the sole descendants and the true heirs of the Star People. And they were ready and willing to go to any lengths necessary to reclaim their fictitious Golden Age.

Sentience Reborn

If any sort of historical categorisation can be imposed on the history of post-human Mankind, the post-Qu era of emerging human animals can be considered a series of dark ages. However, like any 'dark age' situation, these periods of silence had finite lifespans. One by one, like stars emerging from fog, new civilisations were born out of the shattered remnants of Mankind.

In some rare cases, the recovery was swift and straightforward. In most others, it came only after a lengthy series of adaptive radiations, extinctions and secondary diversifications. Within these lines of descent, there was as much distance between the early, scurrying mammals and *Homo sapiens* itself.

Sooner or later, human intelligence returned to the cosmos. However, apart for their shared ancestry, these new people had nothing in common with the 'people' of today, or even each other.

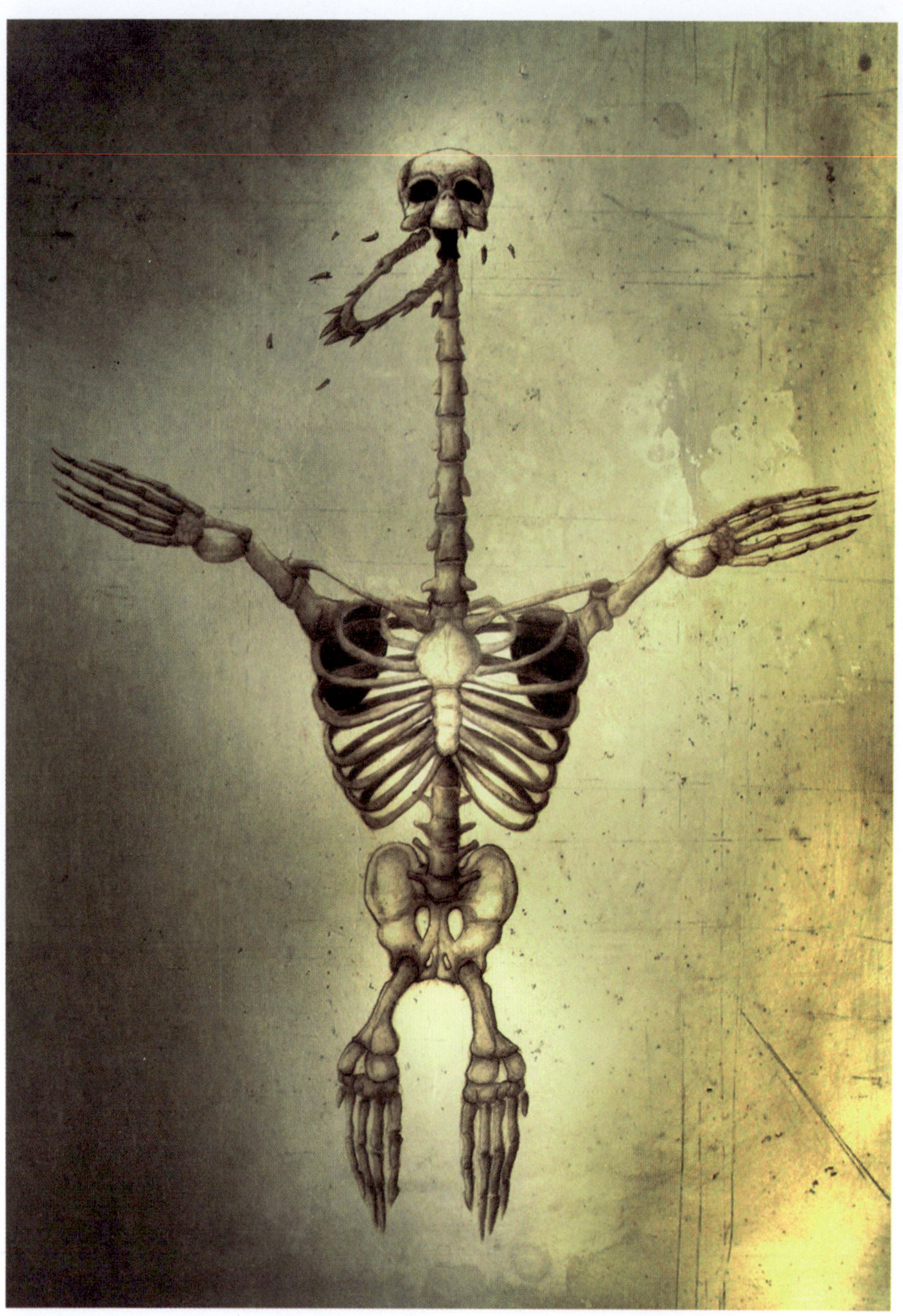

The fossil of an extinct, aquatic human from a forgotten colony world. Unbeknownst to the universe, his kind adapted, flourished and died out soon after the Qu retreat. His tale serves to remind us that all that is alive will inevitably perish, and it is the journey, not the conclusion, that matters.

Extinction

Not all human animals made it through. In fact, it must be realised that the *majority* of post-Qu humans died out during the eras of transition. Extinction – the utter and absolute death of an entire family, entire community, entire species – was rampant in the galaxy.

There was nothing cruel or dramatic about all of this. Extinction was as common and as natural as speciation. Sometimes a species simply failed to adapt to competition or to an abrupt change in conditions. Elsewhere, their numbers dwindled across imperceptible gulfs of time. One way or another, human animals faded out.

In among all of this death, however, there was new life. As one species vacated a certain niche, others would soon step in to take its place. Adaptive radiations would follow, filling in the blanks with myriad diverse and varied forms. Despite the fallen, the flow of life would proceed, blazing with constant replacement.

A Snake Person at home, enjoying a book while smoking and 'listening' to vibrational ground-music.

Snake People
(Descendants of the Worms)

The scorching sun eventually cooled down, and life flooded back to the surface of their world from its subterranean stronghold. Just as animals of all kinds exploded into the terrestrial niches that had been left vacant for millennia, so did the descendants of the Worms. On the surface, they found new opportunities as entire assemblages of serpentine grazers, swimmers, predators . . . and people.

One form, descended from tree-climbing mammalian snakes, re-evolved the human intelligence that had lain dormant for so long. It observed, contemplated and philosophised with novel, spirally coiled brains and manipulated the world with a singular pelvic 'hand' borne from the remnants of its ancestors' feet.

The Snake People looked nothing at all like their distant human ancestors, but their social development followed a similar path: several agricultural world empires, followed by industrial revolutions, social experiments, world wars, civil wars and globalisation. But then again, socio-political parallelism in history did not necessarily imply a similar, or even recognisably human world.

Modern cities of the global Snake world were tangles of pipe-like 'roads', branching, three-dimensional railways and windowless, hole-like buildings. Though their knotted architecture differed from region to region, these settlements generally looked like enormous tangles of glass, metal, plastic and cloth, wrapped so tightly that a human of today would find it impossible to move inside them. Plazas and open areas were totally absent, as they presented navigational obstacles and areas of insecurity. Their evolutionary background in the trees had turned the Snake People into borderline agoraphobes.

None of these, of course, was unusual to the Snakes in any way. Their relatively 'alien' lifestyle was as particular to them as ours is to us. All across their world, the arterial cities throbbed with people, each with their own joys, sorrows and chores, living out lives as human as any other intelligent being's.

A young male Killer tours one of the myriad ruined fortresses in his country, testament to their species' bloody, Protean history. The planet of the Killer Folk is an archaeologist's paradise. It has more buried dark ages, ruined cultures and fallen kingdoms than any other world.

Killer Folk
(Descendants of the Predators)

The predators also rebounded into civilisation. Their journey involved a series of changes during which they lost the adaptations that had allowed them to endure as the top predators of their world. The sabre teeth, once used for slashing through sinew and trachea, became fragile and thin, useful only as organs of social display. The hook-like thumb-claws were also reduced, but not deleted. The last two digits rotated perpendicularly to become newfangled graspers. These specialisations, however, did not mean a decrease in strength. Although they were no longer specialised for hunting, the Killer Folk could still kill with their bare hands, but only if they really wanted to. What enormous claws and teeth could not do, they could easily achieve with bow and arrow, flintlock repeater or gas rifle.

Being descended from predators gave the Killer Folk a unique social profile. Almost all of their religions had rituals allowing for periods of completely natural, animalistic hunts and duels. The necessity of venting these atavistic urges also led to the formation of religious 'hunter nobilities' – privileged warriors who were skilled in the arts of hunting, war and murder. Entire societies were assembled underneath these ruling classes – orderly communities that erupted once every year into an orgy of prayer, sex and death. For thousands of years, nomadic warriors, together with their vast herds of once-human livestock, chased and battled each other across a chessboard of continents.

All of this chaos was to be swept away with the advent of modernity. In a development comparable to an industrial revolution, one nation pack of Killers devised methods of settled, intensive factory farming. Organised state structure, secularism and technological leap-frogging were quick to follow.

Needless to say, such developments polarised the world into bands of progressive, developed 'factory herders' and increasingly fanatical 'hunting states'. While one side condemned old, animal ways, the other side embraced them with blind zealotry. This was their crisis of modernity – the balkanisation of the progressive and conservative factions on the road to global unity. Fortunately, the Killers managed to pull through, even though they drifted dangerously close to global conflict at certain points.

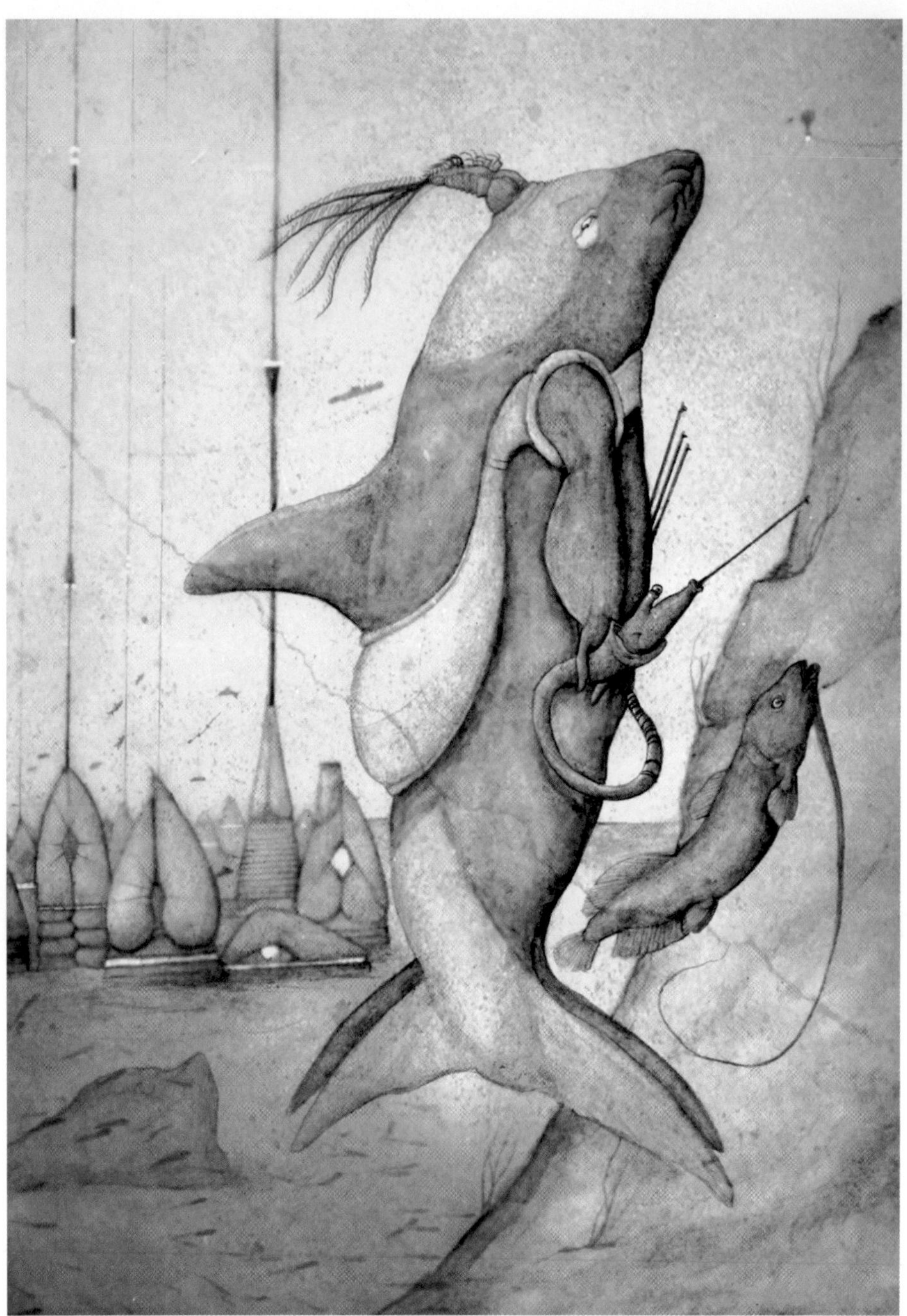

A Tool Breeder huntress on a garden reef. Living tools were an indispensable part of these beings' daily lives; here she manages to breathe underwater through an oxygen-filtering crustacean fitted over her blowhole. She holds a mollusc-derived rifle that shoots out specially modified fish teeth, and her companion is a brain-augmented fish that has been hardwired to return kills. Buildings made from calcified shells glitter in the background, ablaze with bioluminescence.

Tool Breeders
(Descendants of the Swimmers)

They used to be simple creatures, descendants of a battered people that had taken to the sea. Their remote *sapiens* ancestors would have given such beings no chance of a sentient comeback, for they thought that technological advances were impossible in the fluid medium of the oceans. But the Swimmers disproved such beliefs by founding one of the most advanced and most outrageously alien cultures of the entire human lineage.

Fire, the cornerstone of industrial engineering, was almost impossible to sustain and use underwater. But the Tool Breeders simply chose another path when complex tool-making proved impracticable. They began to *breed* their tools and machines for themselves.

It had started long before the species was even intelligent. Of the endless variety of life in the seas, the Swimmers had always adopted and controlled any organisms that were useful in some way. Once domesticated, these creatures were willingly or unintentionally modified through artificial selection and conditioning. The process was slow, but once underway, its effects were formidable.

A modern Tool Breeder city was a sight to behold. Huge, heart-like creatures pumped out nutritious fluids to a network of self-repairing, living conduits. This was their equivalent of a power grid, and it reached each one of the Breeders' huge, exoskeletal dwellings – 'powering' bioluminescent lights, flickering cephalopod-skin televisions, medicinal sea-squirts and countless other devices that had been bred from living creatures. The advances in biology had risen exponentially, until genetic engineering was completely mastered. Modern Breeders did not even need to use animals; a simple manipulation of cultured tissues and stem cells could offer solutions to any problem at hand.

The mastery of genetics had allowed the Tool Breeders to conquer many obstacles. The yawning ocean depths, as well as the planet's few tiny landmasses, were now firmly within the Breeders' grasp. However, they were not content with mere planetary dreams. New forms of living tools and bizarre creatures were still being developed, in daring attempts to conquer the one realm that was most hostile to life.

Sealed in their living ships, the Tool Breeders wished to return to the stars.

A Saurosapient and its trusty steed.

Saurosapients
(Livestock of the Lizard Herders)

One of humanity's eventual inheritors was not even human. It derived from the reptilian stock that had proliferated during the demise of the Lizard Herders.

Theirs was a true case of a world turned upside down. As the humans degenerated into witless animals, the cold-blooded reptiles prospered in the tropical climate of their planet. Generations passed and they began to evolve into increasingly smarter forms, one of which, distantly resembling featherless versions of the predatory dinosaurs of the past, actually crossed over the threshold of sentience and built up a series of civilisations.

These fledgling cultures began to understand the true origin of the monstrous ruins littering their planet, ruins that until then had been considered natural aberrations or timeless memorabilia of gods. Now, however, they saw the intermingled ruins of the Qu and the Star People for what they really were. It was through this understanding that the biologically unrelated Saurosapients nevertheless took up the cultural identity of humanity.

In their archaeological efforts, the Saurosapients began to understand that the animals they used for food and labour were descended from the founders of their very existence. And somewhere in the stars lurked the forces that malformed them, forces greater than the Star People, dark forces that might some day return. The human animals served as a reminder, just as *Panderavis* had to the Star People, that if the Saurosapients wanted to assure their continued existence in the cosmos they had to be watchful.

The pressure of such a reality put their cultures under enormous stress. Some factions turned to religions and remained ignorant under an umbrella of comforting fantasies. Others acknowledged the threats of the galaxy, but reverted to a paranoid rhetoric of conservationism; the galaxy had scared them greatly. Finally, there were those who saw the galactic redoubt and acted to face the odds, however great they might be. Conflicts and even wars were not uncommon between these three factions.

In the end, the centuries-long dispute began to resolve in the progressive factions' favour. As they expanded their spheres of knowledge, influence and activity, the Saurosapients became as 'human' as any other civilisation opening up to the galaxy.

A Modular colony treats a specialised digester unit with sprays of anti-ulcer medication produced by the medical drone held in its 'hands'. Note the differing segments, each one a mutated human being.

Modular People
(Descendants of the Colonials)

The blind workings of evolution followed the unlikeliest paths and made use of the most fleeting opportunities. The very existence of the Modular People was testament to this fact. Their ancestors, the Colonials, would have been seen as hopeless cases by almost any observer; they lacked coherent organs and their existence was limited to carpeting water shores like mats of algae. But as degenerate as they were, the Colonials were resilient survivors, able to hold on to life in the harshest of conditions.

As time passed, they began to organise themselves in differentiated colonies instead of homogenous mats. In the colonies, each human 'cell' could perform a singular function and benefit from union with others. Thus began the great age of organisation, during which colonies competed with each other by developing specialised human cells that would give them an edge in the struggle for life. Some colonies grew enormous taproots that were able to siphon resources from far away. Others abandoned roots altogether and began to move themselves on motile foot segments. Some colonies came up with units equipped with claws and poisons, taking competition to a brand-new, deadly level. Others responded to the threat with armour plating or watcher cells equipped with enormous eyes.

The eventual winner of this Colonial arms race was a sentient colony, organised around hyperspecialised units whose entire purpose was to direct the others. These colonies spread around the planet as they adapted parts of their rivals to function within themselves. Thus were the Modular People born.

Living in fully industrialised megalopoli, they came in an indescribable variation of shapes and sizes; anything from a castle-like guardian forest to a diminutive, scuttling courier was a member of the Modular Whole. They could combine with each other and split up, or exchange parts when the need arose. The only constant in all of their Protean existence was their mental and cultural unity.

Due to their biological structure, these people had managed the impossible. They were living in a world of peace and utopian equality, where everybody was happy to be part of one or other greater, united whole.

A Pterosapiens poses by the bizarre buildings of a seaside resort. At ten days long, this will have been the only holiday in her ephemeral life.

Pterosapiens
(Descendants of the Flyers)

The Flyers' supercharged hearts had given them an evolutionary winning hand, and they diversified to fill up the heavens. It was only a matter of time before the competition in the skies got too intense, even for their enhanced metabolisms.

Some lineages gave up their wings and returned to the ground, living as differing sorts of predators, herbivores and even swimmers. Their aerial adaptations gave them an edge on the ground and they produced forms of stupendous size and agility. There were wonderful creatures, but no sentience came out of the terrestrial sky-beasts. Instead, civilisation flowered in the skies. One species, from a line of wading, stork-like predators, evolved a brain that was large enough to imagine and act upon the world. Their feet, already versatile and used to catch slippery, swamp-dwelling prey, became even more articulate and assumed the role of hands. As a trade-off, they lost some of their aerial streamlining, but what they could not do with their bodies they were more than able to make up for with their minds.

The power of flight made the Pterosapiens a global folk, before they could invent nations and borders. With such an inherent ease of travel, ideas and individuals diffused too quickly for social differences to ossify into mutually hostile cultures. Acting with a planetary awareness, they farmed their gigantic, terrestrial relatives, raised cities of perches and fluted towers, harnessed the atom and began to gaze up into the heavens. With their egalitarian society, they were able to develop a sophisticated civilisation without having to compensate for individual liberties.

Their biology, in retaining flight, had given them an egalitarian society. But also through it, they paid an inevitably limiting price. The Pterosapiens's heart, even in its boosted state, had trouble supporting its power of flight and grotesquely large brains at the same time. As a consequence, the species had an ephemeral lifespan. A Pterosapiens was sexually mature at two, middle-aged by sixteen and usually dead by twenty-three years of their world. This grim cycle caused them to appreciate every moment of their existence dearly, and they pondered upon it with feverish intensity. A shelf of scrolls by Pterosapiens philosophers would have been the envy of every human library. In their cities, life blazed away with unreal speed, rushing past to meet fleeting deadlines.

As a species, the angelic Flyers were often victims of heart disease.

An Asymmetric nobleman poses nude to reveal his bizarre anatomy. Normally, these beings dressed up in elaborate garments that resembled heaps of interconnected cloth tubes.

Asymmetric People
(Descendants of the Lopsiders)

Although contorted by gravity, the Lopsiders managed to regain their sentience and develop a civilisation in a few million years. Squat, pancake-like buildings spread all over their planet. These constructs looked like squashed bunkers, and they were never more than a few metres high. They did not seem like much, but such structures were entrances to underground homes, schools, hospitals, temples and universities, as well as embassies, prisons, asylums, command centres and arsenals. They lived strange lives, but the Lopsiders were human in all of their virtues and evils. Thus, it was only natural for them to expand outwards and look for new frontiers to colonise. Fortunately, their solar system harboured other planets, similar to the Lopsiders' home-world in almost all respects – with the exception of gravity, which was far lower, and thus more conducive to the development of an advanced civilisation.

Throughout their history, humans had always risked changing themselves to preserve their future. It was a risky gamble, but it had paid off since the days of the Martians. But re-engineering the flattened Lopsider body for lower gravity was a monumental task indeed. Suffice to say it took generations of experimentation on their own kind to achieve even limited success. After countless attempts, the Asymmetric People were born – or rather, made. Their bodies had been changed considerably: what had been shovel-like toes for slithering along high-gravity ground had become centipedal legs, and the singular grasping hand was elongated to an extreme degree. Their grotesque faces had been inverted and turned upside-down after reverting from a flounder-like existence. Twisted as they were, members of this new race enjoyed tremendous advantages over their flattened forebears.

Their social development also parallelled that of the bygone Martians, all the way back in Mankind's own solar system. Once again there was a golden age, followed by increasing tensions and interplanetary war. But unlike the Martians, the Asymmetrics ruthlessly exterminated their parent race and went on to rule the solar system alone. On the way, they stumbled across the remains of the Qu and the Star People and advanced immensely. Triumphant within their own realm, they turned to the heavens for further exploits.

A Symbiote poses on one of his several hosts. In the background can be seen some of the Symbiotes' rural housing, with tall doors for the mindless hosts and smaller holes for their intelligent patrons.

Symbiotes
(Descendants of the Parasites)

As time passed, the relationships between the Parasites and their hosts became so strong that they began to involve a true cooperation between individuals. These were no longer one-sided relationships; in exchange for the hosts' nutritious blood, the Parasites offered their heightened senses as early warning against predators and other hazards.

A great 'arms race' of symbiotic relationships thus commenced. Certain Parasites offered their hosts larger eyes, others sharper senses of smell or hearing, or even additional defensive weapons such as venomous saliva, malodorous sprays or an extra bite. The hosts returned the favour with longer running legs, stronger bodies or specialised, ergonomic nesting sites rich in blood vessels and covered in insulating fur. Different complexes of Parasite and host species evolved, compatible only between themselves.

The development of such creatures was in a way reminiscent of the great Modular colonies, thriving on their own world light-years away. But unlike the Modulars, which were modified variations of the same basic organism, the components of the Symbiotes belonged to different species. In any event, both relationships led to the same point: sentience.

In the secluded forests of one particular continent, a new parasitic species developed. They did not have the ballistic poison sprays, infectious stings or grossly hypertrophied arm-claws of their relatives. Instead, these Parasites offered a simpler bargain: an ability to think in return for total submission. Initially this relationship was like that of a mount and its rider, but after a few thousand generations, the Symbiotes could manipulate their hosts like puppets through a combination of tactile and olfactory signals.

More time passed and these combined beings developed a world order unlike our own, complete with countries, politics and even war, albeit reduced in the newly globalised world-culture. In this age, technology filled most functions of the hosts, but a thriving husbandry of these creatures still remained due to tradition and simple efficiency. An average Symbiote would begin the day on his business host, and move on to a more comfortable domestic one when he returned home after work.

And perhaps, on the olfactory television, he would smell news of the excavations of the million-year-old Qu ruins, of the marvellous discoveries salvaged from the Star People wrecks, or of the enormous radio arrays that rose everywhere to listen to the stars.

It was a pattern that was being repeated all over.

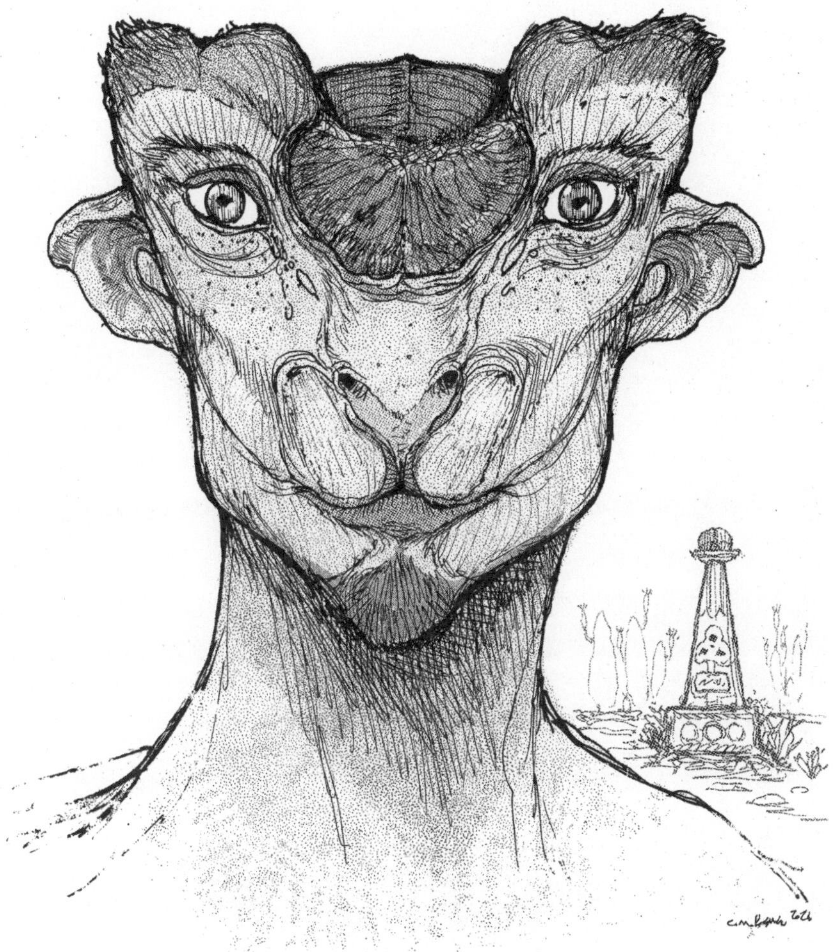

A Host without its Symbiote master will always feel incomplete . . .

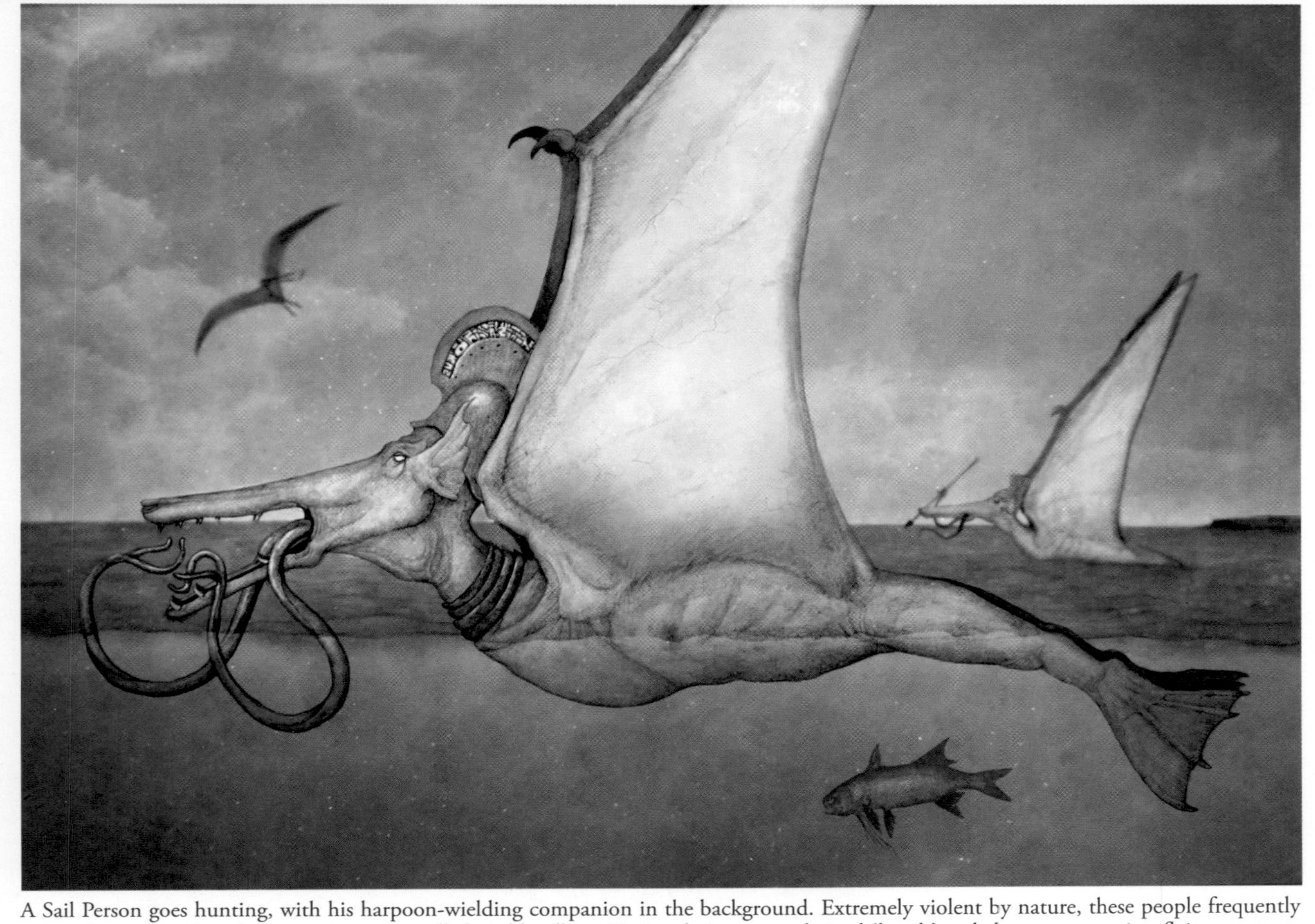

A Sail Person goes hunting, with his harpoon-wielding companion in the background. Extremely violent by nature, these people frequently resorted to savage hunting campaigns to quell their bloodlust. Notice their tongue-derived 'hands' and the accompanying flying creature, actually one of the Sail People's distant cousins.

Sail People
(Descendants of the Finger Fishers)

The Finger Fishers were already among the most divergent of the post-human species. With harpoon-like digits and almost crocodilian muzzles, they looked nothing like their ancestral stock. But even this form would seem conservative to their sentient descendants. With many small, scattered islands, isolated sub-continents and differentiated niches, their home-world was an evolutionary cauldron where isolated members of certain species could, under the right circumstances, evolve into wildly different forms. These conditions were similar to the island realms of Madagascar, Galapagos or Hawaii on old Earth, except that this time it was on a global scale.

Some descendants of the Finger Fishers, trapped on lonely islands, grew smaller and their fishing claws developed into graceful wings. Others took directly to the sea and became the analogues of whales, dolphins and Cretaceous mosasaurs. Within this evolutionary bubble, one particular lineage gave rise to the first Sail People.

Their fingers, too, elongated into wings, but these were not used for flight. Instead, they became sails that drove them effortlessly across the oceans. With their fingers employed for this purpose, they used their mouths and extended tongues to catch their pelagic prey. These organs eventually assumed the role of the Finger Fishers' long, atrophied, dexterous hands. Meanwhile, the need to better navigate the endless seas placed an inevitable demand on their memories, and the Sail People's brains grew correspondingly. It was only a matter of time before one of these navigators became smart enough to think.

Even when sentient, the Sail People still needed a long time to achieve any sort of social stability. Their scattered world made for a tremendous diversity of cultures, which competed and fought relentlessly. Across generations, untold flotillas of tribal warriors battled each other in epoch-spanning, pointless conflicts. Nomadic warriors and pirate societies inevitably came into being, prolonging the uncontrollable cycle of violence.

Only when a certain warrior tribe developed warfare on an industrial scale, along with the society needed to support it – and then, only when this notion of modernity gave rise to an idea of peace – did the Sail People finally manage to unify. Generations of blood had stained the oceans for far too long.

A Satyriac audience goes wild as the performer hits the climax of his song. Such events were part of everyday Satyriac life.

Satyriacs
(Descendants of the Hedonists)

Their pleasure-drenched existence, caught between their static paradise-world and their inherently slow pace of evolution, had made the Satyriacs seem immune to change. Perhaps this was true for some time but on a larger timescale, complete stasis would prove merely a fable.

During one particular era, geological upheavals threw huge masses of land over the shallow oceans of their world. The Hedonists, until then trapped on a single, small island continent, were quick to colonise these new pastures. Their innocence finally spoiled, most of the Hedonists died out, unable to adapt. The only survivors were fast-breeding freaks who had abandoned the reproductive quirks of their ancestors. It was these forms that colonised the newborn continent and gave rise to a multitude of species, which included the Satyriacs, sentient heirs to the Hedonists.

These beings closely resembled their ancestors, except that they now sported enormous 'tails' – boneless organs of balance woven out of extended pelvic muscles and fat. Their entire bodies were reoriented to horizontal postures to accommodate this new organ. Although they had abandoned the frantic reproductive strategies of their ancestors, their social lives still retained a delightful tint of casual promiscuity.

The Satyriac civilisation was quick to establish itself globally. For a while, three and then two land empires competed with each other, before dissolving into myriad smaller nations and finally reunifying into a coherent world order. From this point on, the Satyriac world once again became a paradise of sensations, with festivals, concerts and ritualised orgies punctuating every working week. This time, however, it could all be savoured with true intelligence.

A Bug Facer celebrity, arguably the most beautiful woman on their planet, poses before a coastal village. In the distance can be seen gasbag-like tree creatures, relics of the mysterious alien invaders.

Bug Facers
(Descendants of the Insectophagi)

Over time, the Bug Facers' insectivorous ancestors came to resemble their prey. Hardened, leathery face plates, once used for defence against stings and bites, ossified and became integrated into the jaw structure. Their hands and feet, with reduced numbers of fingers and toes, developed into pincer-like affairs. Even their metabolism reverted partially to ectothermy in the balmy, lazy climate of their planet.

But it was none of those adaptations that gave them the edge in survival. Simply put, a congenital defect allowed them to regain their sentience. Even after the stunting of their minds by the Qu, the genes of the Star People remained dormant in their cells. Through pure coincidence, one lineage of the Insectophagi developed an atavistic throwback resulting in larger brains, which just happened to be useful for cracking open insect nests with crude stone tools.

Things advanced rapidly after that. Although millennia-long in itself, the Bug Facers' development from stone axe to spaceship was over in an eye-blink in geological time. Like many other species, they passed through consecutive cycles of agrarian (in their case hive-farming) empires, colonial endeavours, industrialisation, massive world wars and finally, globalised world-states. But there was one thing that set their development apart from all other post-human species: they faced another alien invasion.

History does not record much about the invaders, except that, unlike the Qu, theirs was a one-off effort and was beaten off in an intense cycle of orbital and terrestrial wars. Although vanquished, the invaders successfully left their mark on the Bug Facer world. They introduced their own flora and fauna, which flourished on the Bug Facer home planet long after their departure. More importantly, they imbued the Bug Facers with a pathological inter-species xenophobia, to the point where they were fearful of even their post-human cousins on other stars.

Through an ironic twist of fate, their fears would be more than justified, though not just yet. The Bug Facers still had time.

Asteromorphs
(Descendants of the Spacers)

Initially refugees, the Spacers were quick to master the vastness of interstellar space. Their isolated space arks joined together and multiplied to form a gigantic, interlocked structure that was large enough to contain entire worlds. But no planets lay inside the Asteromorph capital; only cavernous, gravity-free bubbles where the inhabitants could finally develop to their fullest.

Freed from the constraints of weight, their bodies grew spindly and insectile, with individual digits extending into multitudes of thin, versatile limbs. Other than these, the only newly evolved organs were their derived jet-sphincters, which went on to become the principal means of locomotion. But above all were their brains – their bulging, swollen brains.

With no hindrance from gravity, the human brain could grow to unprecedented sizes. Each generation devised experiments that produced offspring with greater cranial capacity, giving rise to beings that spent their everyday lives thinking in concepts and structures scarcely comprehensible to the people of today. The physiological limitations of the human mind had long been debated. Now, it was established that these limits, while real for most, could in fact be broken, and the individuals who achieved this would likewise conquer new grounds in philosophy, art and science.

Yet some aspects of humanity, such as the basic desire to venture forth and explore new realms, remained. To this end the Asteromorphs built great fleets of globular sub-arks and spread their influence across the heavens, into every stellar cluster and every star system. Within less than a thousand years, the galaxy was straddled by a new and far more alien Empire of Asteromorphs.

Strangely enough, its dominion included none of the newly emerging post-human species, for its masters had completely lost interest in planets – those stunted, gravity-chained balls of dirt and ice. The newborn arks settled comfortably in the outer rims of star systems, quietly observing the lives of their struggling relatives.

For the first time in history, there were actual gods in the myriad human skies. They were silent and weren't even noticed most of the time, but their watchfulness would ultimately pay off.

Second Galactic Empire

Over time, the sentient post-humans began to reach out to the rest of the galaxy. They inevitably stumbled across the ruins of the Star People and deduced their interstellar ancestry. These discoveries were followed by a realisation: that there might be others like them, unimaginable distances away. Thus, the fledgling civilisations set about probing the skies.

The contacts, all established by radio communication, were somewhat sporadic. The Second Empire began little more than a few million Earth years after the Qu left, with the first dialogue between the earliest Killer Folk and the Satyriacs. A few thousand years later, they were joined by the Tool Breeders, calling out from the ocean depths through living radio arrays.

The second wave of sentient species joined in over the following 10 million years, as the Modular Whole, Pterosapiens and the fledgling Asymmetrics contacted their celestial cousins. Finally, over the next 20 million years, newly evolving civilisations such as the Saurosapients, Snake People, Parasites/Symbiotes and the Sail People successively contacted the burgeoning Galactic Empire. The Bug Facers were aware of the whole process, but due to their xenophobic experience, they opened up only after a staggering 40 million years of silence.

This union was an empire of speech, for actual travel between the stars was too difficult to be practical. Like the bygone colonies of the Star People, the post-humans co-operated through the unrestricted exchange of information and experience. Although it covered every aspect of an astonishing variety of cultures, the Empire's efforts focused on two main issues: political unification (though not homogenisation) and galactic awareness – constant readiness for possible alien invasions. Everybody had come across the remains of the mysterious Qu. Nobody wanted a repeat of the same scenario.

When the Second Empire ran into the Asteromorphs (who had silently saturated the galaxy with their own empire), they feared the worst. But luckily for them, the godlike beings were not interested in the Second Empire, nor any of its worlds. The Asteromorphs were given a wide berth and accepted as they were: incomprehensible, omnipotent forces of nature.

This coordinated effort lasted almost 80 million years, during which its member species attained previously unimaginable levels of culture, welfare and technology. Each species colonised a few dozen worlds of their own, in which nations, cultures and individuals lived to achieve the fullest potential of their existence.

Needless to say, all of this was possible only through constant communication and a total openness to the galaxy. Most communities took this for granted and dutifully participated in the galactic conversation. But there were others – silent, darkened beings – who refused to join in. Through them would come the ruin of the Empire.

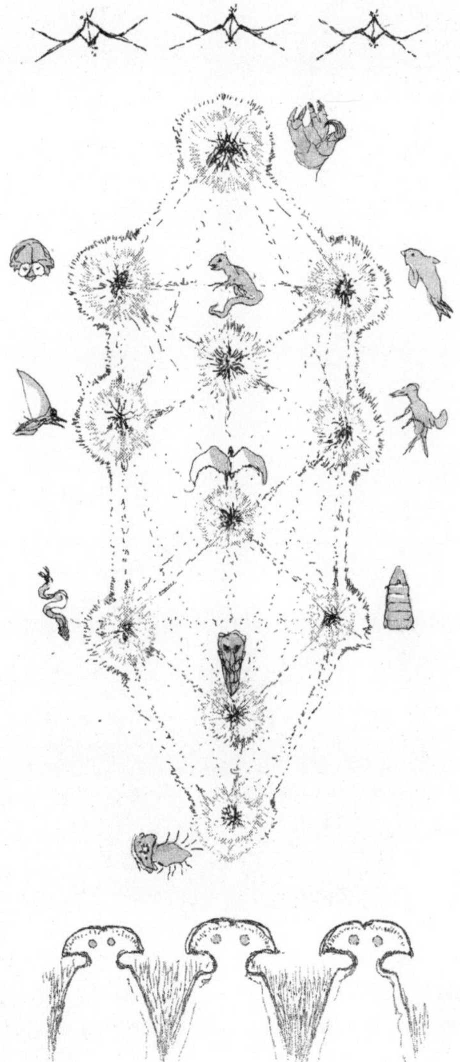

This diagram of the 'Image of Humanities' was a potent symbol of the Second Galactic Empire immediately before the Gravital onslaught.

All member races were arrayed as idealised distillations of their species' ethos, reaching above from Fear, Love, and Hunger – the three main forces that drive all life; to the star-like ideals of Truth, Beauty and Power – representing the ultimate Image of Humanity.

From the bottom to the top, left to right they are: the Asymmetric People, embodying resilience; the Snake People, embodying wisdom; the Insectophagi, embodying secrecy and caution; the Modular People, embodying constant endurance and victory; the Sail People, embodying severity; the Pterosapiens, embodying splendour and majesty; the Hedonists, embodying joy, mercy and procreation; the Symbiotes, embodying intelligence and guidance; the Saurosapiens, embodying willpower and acceptance; the Tool breeders, embodying the seeding of life; and the Killer Folk, embodying mastery and resurgence.

Gravital
(Descendants of the Ruin Haunters)

After the lesson of the Qu, the Second Galactic Empire kept a constant watch against alien invasion. Yes, naively, they neglected to look among themselves. The second great invasion of the galaxy came not from outside, but from within.

The Ruin Haunters, who were lucky enough to inherit the secrets of the Star People and the Qu when other species were mere animals, had experienced a tremendous advance in technological prowess. All in all, they were as sophisticated as, if not more than, the Asteromorphs of the void. But their own ascendancy was not a sane one. Remember that most Ruin Haunters were already deranged, with a twisted assumption of being the sole inheritors of the Star People. They refused to communicate with their relatives on other planets, and kept to their own affairs. This neurotic hubris assumed truly dangerous proportions after the Ruin Haunters modified themselves.

The origin of this modification lay in an earlier catastrophe. The Ruin Haunters' sun was undergoing a rapid phase of expansion, and the species, advanced as it was, could do nothing to stop the process. So the Haunters did the next best thing, and changed their bodies.

The infernal conditions of the solar expansion meant that a biological reconstruction was totally out of the question. Instead, the Haunters replaced their bodies with machines – floating spheres of metal that moved and moulded their environment through subtle manipulations of gravity fields. In earlier versions, the spheres still cradled the organic brains of the last Haunters. But in successive generations, ways of containing the mind within quantum computers were devised, and the transformation became absolute. Their self-modification now complete, the Ruin Haunters turned into the completely mechanical Gravital. While not even organic, the Gravital retained human dreams, human ambitions and human delusions of grandeur. This, combined with mechanical bodies that allowed them to cross space with ease, made interstellar war a frightening possibility.

A rare instance of a direct invasion by the Gravital, on one of the coastal cities of the Killer Folk. Most of the time, the citizens of the Second Empire were wiped out in a single global event, without the necessity for such confrontations.

Machine Invasion

It took a long time for the Gravital to prepare. Propulsion systems were perfected and new bodies, capable of withstanding the interstellar jumps, were devised. But when they finally decided that the time was nigh, *nothing* survived their slaughter.

The invasions followed a brutally simple plan. The target worlds' suns were blockaded and their light was blocked by enormous, artificial screens. If the dying worlds managed to resist, an asteroid or two finished them off. Enormous invasion fleets were built, but it was rarely necessary to deploy them. The Gravital had caught their cousins completely off guard.

The Great Dyings, all of which occurred over a relatively quick, 10,000-year period, stretched the boundaries of genocide and horror. Almost all of the new human species – unique beings who had endured mass extinctions, navigated evolutionary knife-edges and survived to build worlds of their own – vanished without a trace.

Even the Qu had been loyal to life; they had distorted and subjugated their victims, but in the end they had allowed them to survive. To the machines, however, life was a luxury.

Ironically, such thorough ruthlessness was not borne of any kind of actual hatred. The Gravital, long accustomed to their mechanical bodies, simply did not acknowledge the life of their organic cousins. When this apathy was mixed with their un-sane claims to be the sole heirs of the Star People, the extinctions were carried out with the banality of, say, an engineer tearing down an abandoned building. Under the reign of the machines, the galaxy entered a new dark age.

When Considering the Invasion

The Machine Invasion brought on the greatest wave of extinctions the galaxy had ever seen, for it was not a simple act of war by one species against another, but a systematic destruction of life itself.

When considering such a vast event, it is easy to get lost in romantic delusions. It is almost as easy to write off the Gravital as 'evil' as it is to consider the entire episode as a nihilistic, 'end of everything' kind of scenario. Both of these approaches are, as they would be in any historical situation, monumental fallacies.

To begin with, the Gravital were not evil, at least not by their own measure. These beings, although mechanical, still lived their lives as individuals and operated inside coherent societies. They had surrendered their organic heritage but their minds were not the cold, calculating engines of true machines. Even after giving orders that would destroy a billion souls, a Gravital would have a home to go to, and, as incredibly as it might sound, a family and a circle of friends towards which it felt genuine affection. As mentioned before, despite being endowed with compassion, the Gravital's harsh treatment of the organics was the result of a simple inability to understand their right to live.

Furthermore, the Gravital did not constitute a singular, indivisible whole whose entire purpose was to wreck the universe. True, their technological advancement had allowed them to form a pan-galactic entity, but within itself the Machine Empire was divided into political factions, even religious faiths. Superimposed over these fault lines were the daily lives and personal affairs of families and individuals. Like any sentient being, they had a sense of identity, and thus, differing agendas.

Nor did the Machine invasion mean the end of everything. There was certainly a widespread destruction of life, but what was lost was 'only' organic life. Consuming energy, directing it to reproduction, thought and even evolution, the machines were as alive as any carbon-based organism. Despite the takeover, a life of sorts survived, and as would be seen, even preserved some of its organic predecessors.

The Bug Facer archetype, flanked by two of his twisted descendants: to his left, a phallus-bearing Polydactyl, bred as a sacrificial offering in one of the many different Machine religions; to the right, a one-off work of art designed to play its modified fingers like a set of drums while ululating the tune of a particular pop song.

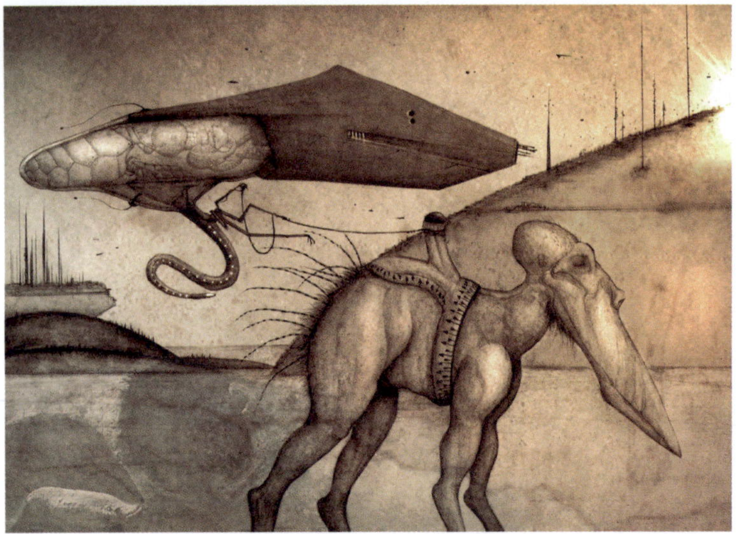

Towards the height of their reign, the machines themselves evolved into numerous diverse forms quite distant from their sphere-shaped Gravital ancestors. The Subject pet paraded by this particular machine citizen has had its face elongated and broadened into a grim imitation of its master.

Subjects
(Many Descendants of the Bug Facers)

The Bug Facers – xenophobic due to their experience of repeated alien invasions – were the first species to face the Gravital onslaught. As ironic as their fate seemed, the Bug Facers were the luckiest of the post-humans. Instead of being exterminated like the rest of their cousins, they survived as the only organic beings in the Machine Empire.

The precise reasons for their retention remain unknown to this day. Perhaps the Gravital hadn't yet perfected their ruthless disregard for organic life. Or perhaps, perplexingly against their latter modus operandi, they took pity to these poor organics and allowed them to maintain a limited parody of existence.

Whatever the reason, the Bug Facers endured, though they barely resembled their original ancestors. Genetic engineering and the modification of living beings – once a lost art, known only to the Qu – was mastered almost as comprehensively by the Gravital. Not hesitating to warp the beings that they did not really consider to be alive, they spliced their way into the Bug Facer DNA, producing generations of literal abominations. Would a woman or man of today show any apprehension towards reassembling a computer, or even recycling trash? Such was the attitude of the triumphant Gravital.

Thus, multitudes of Subjects were produced, distorted to such an extent that even the meddling of the Qu seemed comparatively timid. Most of them were used as servants, caretakers and manual labourers. These were the lucky forms. Some sub-men were reduced to the level of cell cultures, useful only for gas exchange and waste filtering. Others were moulded into completely artificial ecologies – baroque simulations that served only as entertainment. Some Gravital, with their still-human ambitions, took this practice to a new level and produced living works of art: doomed, one-off creatures that existed purely as biological anachronisms.

Be it as tool, slave or entertainment, humanity narrowly held on to its biological heritage while its machine cousins reigned supreme for interminable aeons.

The Other Machines

Remember that despite its galaxy-cradling might, the Machine Empire was not homogenous. It contained dozens of differing factions that did not always agree on everything, including the treatment of their downtrodden, biological Subjects.

Some Gravital, via a process involving several religious, social and philosophical doctrines, began to comprehend the universality of life, and the common origin of organic and mechanical humanities. Initially such individuals lived in seclusion or withheld their beliefs from the world. They secretly engineered lineages of Subjects that could live, move and think as freely as they could themselves. In a few memorable instances, the engineers fell in love with their creations, and were punished by their community for the unthinkable act of showing mercy to an organic servant. Their martyrdom inspired other Gravital to think just a little differently.

Eventually, the ideology gained enough momentum to be practised openly in everyday life. However, the sect of Toleration found itself at odds with its hardline, pan-mechanical rival. The seething intolerance between the two factions finally erupted when some Tolerant Gravital wanted to set several worlds aside for the unrestricted development of biological life. All hell broke loose and the Machine Empire – the apparently seamless monolith of the galaxy – experienced its first civil war, which was short but bitter.

The war did not cause any lasting damage, but it plainly illuminated one fact: the greatest polity the galaxy had ever seen was not without its problems.

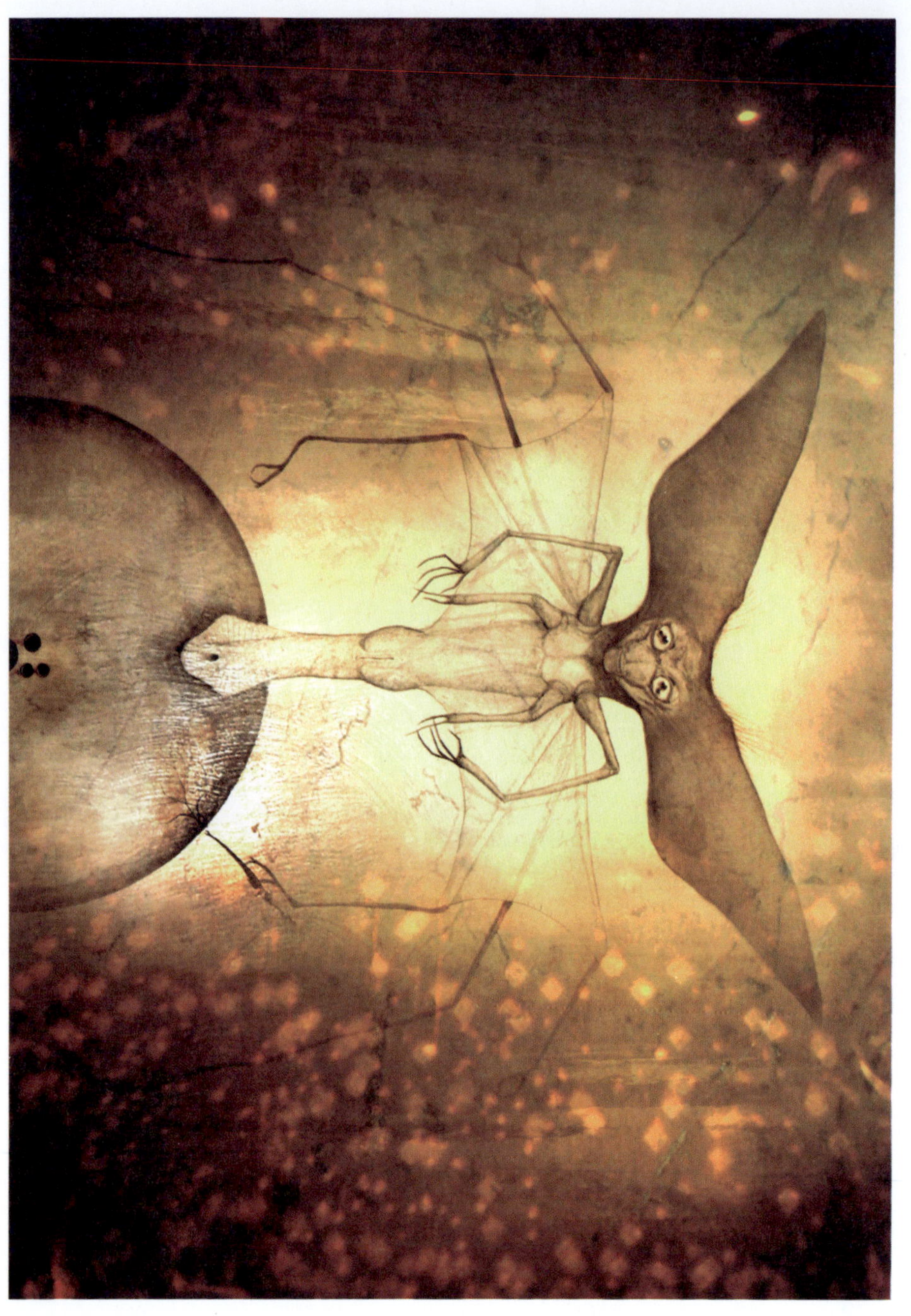

The Fall of the Machines
(Return of the Spacers)

In the long run, the internal struggles of the Machine Empire just *might* have led to its downfall. But there was no need to wait that long, as the Empire died an earlier but immensely more cataclysmic death.

For a long time, the Machine and Asteromorph empires had been eyeing each other nervously. They hadn't yet run into open confrontation, as the Asteromorphs kept mostly to their outer-space arks and the Machine Empire occupied the planets. In almost every inhabitable solar system of the galaxy, the same upside-down tension built up between organic beings living in the void and machines inhabiting perfectly terrestrial worlds.

Power was evenly balanced between the two rival empires. Moreover, this balance involved forces strong enough to destroy whole planets. Each side knew that any kind of war would result in mutual annihilation, and only insanity could start such a conflict.

Well, the post-civil-war empire of the Machines did go insane, in a sense. In order to divert attention from internal struggles, it decided it needed a new enemy against which to consolidate its rival factions. This was an unwise decision, as this enemy came to be the Asteromorphs.

It is unnecessary and in any case nearly impossible to describe the carnage that followed. The conflict lasted several million years, and the resulting loss of life (both mechanical and organic) made the genocides during the initial invasion of the Gravital seem irrelevant.

When the cosmic dust settled, the winners displayed themselves. The conquerors were the Asteromorphs, changed beyond recognition after aeons of continual self-perfection. Their grossly hypertrophied brains stretched out like wings on either side of their heads and their finger-derived limbs formed an intricate set of sails and legs. Endowed with superior technology and limitless patience, these beings almost completely destroyed the Gravital, despite losing a substantial number of their own species.

The conflict also thrust the Asteromorphs into the affairs of their long-neglected human cousins. As impossible as it seemed, some of the machines' Subjects had survived the ordeal. Now, the Asteromorphs could no longer look away.

With the Gravital gone, it was up to the Asteromorphs to clean up after them. They took up the Subjects and used their genetic heritage to populate entire planets. During this age of reconstruction, which lasted for another million generations, many Asteromorph world-builders emerged as true gods, creating inhabited worlds almost from scratch. The Subjects, meanwhile, became the inheritors of a truly new, if war-torn, phoenix of a galaxy.

A late-stage Gravital pleads for mercy, even as it holds a live Subject captive in its body. How they struggled . . . how they pleaded . . . and, in the end, *how they died*!

A nude Terrestrial shows the highly divergent yet still bizarrely human anatomy that is characteristic of this species. These particular Terrestrials maintained a religious hegemony over their clueless subjects, dressing up in elaborate veils and headgear to assert their 'divine' inheritance.

The Post-War Galaxy

When replenishing lost worlds, the Asteromorph Gods also took measures to ensure the continued safety of their creations. The abrupt rise of the Machines had shown that, unless carefully regulated, the abundance of stars could always host a race of pan-galactic usurpers.

The Asteromorphs, watchful yet hesitant to involve themselves in the affairs of planet-living beings, did not want to interfere directly. Instead, they produced terrestrial versions of their own kind to regulate the galaxy. They adapted their delicate, ethereal fingers into spidery limbs, and shrunk their brains considerably to readjust to the rigours of gravity. The resulting sideline was stunted by Asteromorph standards, but still produced demigods in every sense of the word.

These beings, often known as Terrestrial Spacers or simply Terrestrials, nurtured and controlled the development of the post-war civilisations on many planets. They acted as caretakers, prophets, kings and emperors, but also as grim reapers, as the occasion dictated.

The endeavour did not always proceed as smoothly as planned, of course. Most of the time the newborn races refused to heed their mentors and, in several cases, even rebelled against them. Needless to say, this crime was always punished with a swift extinction. Furthermore, even the Terrestrials grew corrupt. Instead of offering guidance, Terrestrials on many planets simply played God, weaving contrived religions around themselves to shamelessly exploit their subjects. It was not ethical or even productive, but this method seemed to guarantee more stability than actually trying to bring up the new races.

This way or by other means, organic sentience reclaimed its dominance in the galaxy. The New Empire – managed by Terrestrials, populated by myriad descendants of the Subjects, and overseen ultimately by the omniscient Asteromorphs – achieved greater progress and a longer-lasting calm in the galaxy than all of its predecessors combined.

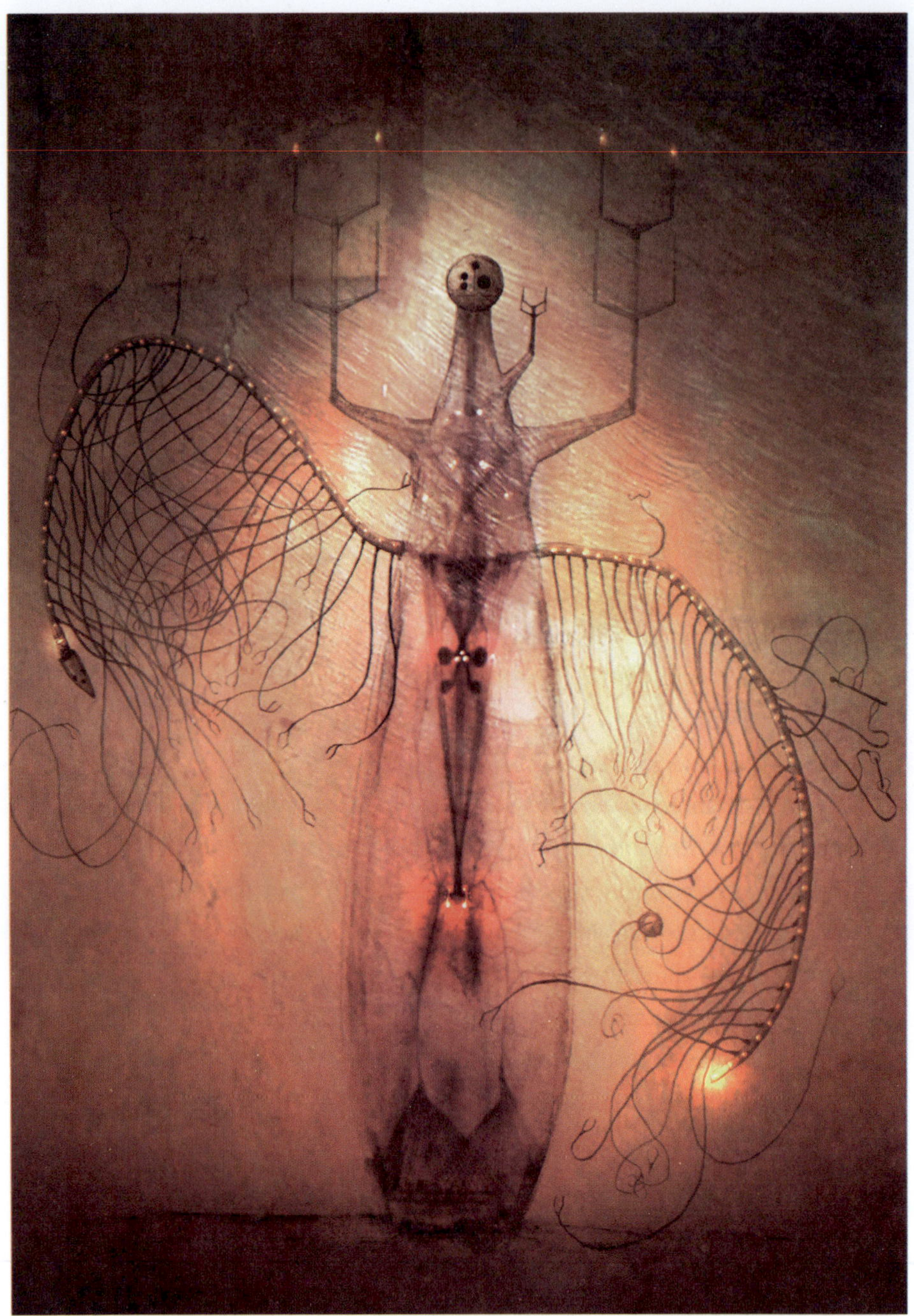

A machine citizen of the New Empire. She sports a dazzling pair of branching arms that suit both the latest fashion trends and her job as an artisan. Machines following fashion might seem unusual to a reader of the current era, but never forget that these beings were human intelligences, just in different bodies.

The New Machines

Long after their fall from grace, the Machines still clung on to existence. In the initial aftermath of the war, the Asteromorphs had planned to exterminate every last one of them, only to discover that the Machines were simply too useful to destroy. For millions of years they had perfected the interface between mind and machine to such an extent that they could live and operate in the most inhospitable conditions. Such beings, deprived of their galaxy-straddling power, would make invaluable contributions to research and exploration in the New Empire.

There was a sense of poetic justice in all of this. The Machines, who once distorted biological life forms on a whim, were finally treated to a similar fate. To begin with, the Asteromorphs completely scrapped their capacity for self-contained gravitational manipulation – the very force that had rendered them invulnerable in the first place. They were given finite lifespans and slightly numbed imaginations, so that history would not repeat itself. The limiting nature of these changes, however, did not entail an overall regression.

Unlike their ancestors, the New Machines were endowed with nanotechnological bodies that could remodel themselves continuously, which meant that they could come in every shape and size imaginable. A New Machine citizen could live for some time in the void of the space, conducting research, and then transform into a completely different body-plan for a holiday on a cometary halo, tropical jungle or methane ocean. He or she could also make the trip personally by growing temporary hyperdrives and ramjet engines.

Despite their breathtaking versatility, the New Machines were never as common or prominent as their original Gravital ancestors, even after completely accepting their role as lowly citizens of the New Empire. The greatest wars in conceivable history had ingrained the organics with too deep a mistrust of their mechanical neighbours, and the New Machines were always treated with a degree of discrimination. The sins of their fathers had come to shackle this most splendorous of all human species.

An Amphicephalus ambassador with spaceships typical of its kind. Her strange body-plan betrays an evolutionary history as complicated as that of humanity.

Second Contact

With successive waves of machine-aided discovery and colonisation, the New Empire grew exponentially. Such was the growth of wealth and progress that their description would require the use of concepts that remain unexplored today. To talk with a person of today about the comings and goings of the New Empire would be akin to giving lectures on twenty-first-century geopolitics to a hunter-gatherer.

The New Empire was not blind to the universe around it. It focused its eyes, ears and other sensors, and probed the events of the surrounding galaxies. The New Galactics suspected that the surrounding nebulae might also house their indigenous folk, and it would be wise to contact them before a misunderstanding or conflict could occur. On a darker side, these observations also served as lookouts for potential invaders. Even then, the memory of the Qu had not been forgotten.

The discovery was eventually made. One of the neighbouring galaxies was showing patterns of activity that matched the unmistakable signs of a sentient organisation. Some thinkers revelled in the discovery of a new civilisation, while others feared a return of the Qu. Fortunately, this second encounter with an alien species proved to be a peaceful one. Perhaps the intelligences of both galaxies were finally great enough to meet without quarrelling.

The other galaxy was dominated by connected unions of different beings, presided over by various kinds of Amphicephali – bizarre creatures that resembled giant serpents with a head at each end, one of which bore a secondary, retractile body that was used to interact with the world. Apparently, the Amphicephali had undergone a series of alternating regressions, evolutionary radiations and self-imposed genetic makeovers, just as humanity had.

With their wild difference, the Amphicephali were welcomed. They were the first, but they were certainly not the last.

By the time Earth was rediscovered, humans had diverged considerably from their ancestral forms.

Earth Rediscovered

The purpose of this work is not to describe the limitless progress that followed the intergalactic contact. One could go on indefinitely, chronicling how the united galaxies re-encountered and subdued the Qu, how they cradled their suns with artificial shells, multiplying their inhabitable zones a billion-fold, how they criss-crossed interstellar space with wormholes and made conventional travel a thing of the past. Ultimately, descendants of those beings conquered even Time itself, indefinitely prolonging the existence of their minds via rejuvenating technologies.

For a time, all humans were gods.

But from today's vantage point, one discovery truly stood out in this orgy of advancement. Compared with gargantuan achievements like the taming of space and the construction of the star-shells, it was a mere blip, a revelation of long-forgotten trivia. It was the rediscovery of Earth – the birthplace of humanity, to which the omnipresent Asteromorphs, the star-gliding Machines and the millions of other galactic races could all trace their origins.

It was made quietly, by a single researcher combing the vestiges of forgotten history – decade after decade. Millions of years of wars, invasions and extinctions had buried the evidence thoroughly and comprehensively. When she finally came across irrefutable evidence, nobody was around to celebrate. That would come later.

The Return

The discovery sparked a certain amount of interest, though nowhere as much as other breakthroughs had. To most humans of the cosmos, their ancestral birthplace was simply an interesting piece of information, a piece of trivia with which they had lost all ties.

Still, a ship was sent forth, and it landed without ceremony, for now there was no intelligence left on Earth. Located too far away from the main zone of human habitation, it had been completely ignored and languished.

When the explorers stepped out onto its surface, human feet trod on old Earth once more, after an absence of 560 million years. Humankind was home.

The author, with a billion-year-old human skull.

All Tomorrows

I must conclude my words with a confession. Mankind, the very species that I've been chronicling, from its terrestrial infancy to its domination of the galaxies, is now extinct. All of the beings that you've seen on the preceding pages – from the lowly Worm to the wind-riding Sail People, from the megalomaniac Gravital to the ultimate Galactic citizens – lie *a billion years* dead. We are only beginning to piece the story together.

Why did Mankind disappear? Perhaps it was a final, unimaginable war of annihilation, one that transcended the very meaning of 'conflict'. Perhaps it was a gradual break-up of the united galaxies, with every race facing their own private end slowly afterwards. Or perhaps, the wildest theories suggest, it was a mass migration to another plane of existence. A journey to somewhere, sometime, *something* else. But the bottom line is: we honestly don't know.

Like every other story, humanity's was a temporary one; long, indeed, but ultimately ephemeral. It did not have a coherent ending – but then again it didn't need to. The story of humanity was never its domination of a thousand galaxies, or its mysterious exit to the unknown. The essence of being human was none of that. Instead, it lay in the radio conversations of the Machines, in the daily lives of the bizarrely twisted Bug Facers, in the endless love songs of the carefree Hedonists, the rebellious demonstrations of the first true Martians, and, in a way, the very life that you, reader, lead at the moment.

Many throughout history were unaware of this most basic fact. The Qu, dreaming of an ideal future, distorted the worlds they came across. Later on, the Gravital, with their insane desire to recreate the past, carried out the biggest massacres in the history of the galaxy. Even now, it is sickeningly easy for beings to get lost in false grand narratives, living out completely driven lives in pursuit of non-existent ultimates, ideals, climaxes and golden ages. In blindly thinking that their stories serve absolute ends, such creatures almost always end up harming themselves, if not those around them.

To those like them: look at the story of Man and come to your senses. It is not the destination but the trip that matters, and what you do today influences tomorrow – not the other way around. Love today, and seize all tomorrows!

Species Commentary

After the initial online release of *All Tomorrows* in 2006, I received numerous questions about what inspired me to design its creatures and characters. Here are brief 'behind-the-scenes' anecdotes for every species in the book.

MARTIANS: this was based on a self-portrait I had done at an earlier date, and its style in the first edition of *All Tomorrows* doesn't match the rest of the artwork. I imagined a leaner version of contemporary humans, with somewhat mixed ethnic characteristics.

STAR PEOPLE: the large-headed humanoid form is a nod to the wise and benevolent alien archetype in popular culture.

PANDERAVIS: the rendering of a dinosaur descendant as a round-bodied, bird-like creature was quite new in its time, in the early 2000s. Interestingly, many discoveries about dinosaur life in the following decades paint a similar picture for some species.

QU: the most iconic species in this book, these beings were inspired by diopsid flies, with their long eyestalks. The arrangement of the wings and tail were almost entirely improvised. In the beginning there was no deep lore behind this species, I just wanted a plot device to make my crazy evolutionary scenarios plausible. Left on their own, star-faring humans would not have devolved into Flyers, Swimmers, etc.; they would have just built planes and boats instead.

WORMS: this was the first image I created for *All Tomorrows* – before I even knew I had a story on my hands. Their body structure is inspired by legless lizards such as *Bipes* and *Dibamus*.

TITANS: this creature was designed around the concept of a post-human with a prehensile lower lip. Initially it was meant to be a more 'regular'-sized being, but I then decided to scale it up – as far as the vertebrate body-plan can go.

PREDATORS AND PREY: these were routine designs for post-humans evolved for a running existence as hunters and grazers. The delicate patterning on the coat of the predators was inspired by Ottoman and Persian hunting miniatures depicting leopards.

MANTELOPES: the form of the Mantelope evolved from a previous, much older sketch (now lost) where human hands and feet were lengthened and contorted to look like the hooves of an antelope. Its long moustache is a homage to iconic Turkish rock singer Barış Manço (1943–1999).

SWIMMERS: many swimming creatures inevitably share the same fish-like body-plan. In designing these swimming post-humans, I wanted to retain this sense of convergent evolution while still creating a relatively original, seal-like leg-fin arrangement.

LIZARD HERDERS: this concept was inspired by my pet iguana at the time of writing. In fact, some of the scales come from photos I took of my iguana.

TEMPTORS: the crazy form of the female Temptor was pure improvisation. There were no sketches or studies – I just drew it on the first attempt.

BONE CRUSHERS: the idea of the teeth forming a beak, as well as this manifesting in a post-human, was inspired by the Pak Protector species in author Larry Niven's Known Space universe.

COLONIALS: the forms of these distorted, brick-like humans were inspired directly by master artist and author Wayne Douglas Barlowe's 'Inferno' series of paintings.

FLYERS: primates and bats are distantly related, so creating this post-human was not a great challenge.

HAND FLAPPERS: this species started out as a joke based on antisocial exhibitionist types. The shape and size of these post-humans' genitalia are actually quite tame compared with the displays of certain primate species living today.

BLIND FOLK: while this was a rigorously scientific design, I also wanted the Blind Folk to resemble the infamous 'Hopkinsville Goblins' in contemporary UFO folklore.

LOPSIDERS: this species came from Pleuronectiform flatfish on our own world. Bit by bit, I reimagined human anatomy, 'flattening' and readapting it for a crawling existence.

STRIDERS: this species was inspired by the attenuated sculptures of the artist Alberto Giacometti (1901–1966).

PARASITES: the Parasites were inspired by desmodontidae vampire bats on our own world. One of my favourite designs.

FINGER FISHERS: the inspiration for this species came not from nature but from my personal memories of looking in rock pools for crabs, starfish and other creatures.

HEDONISTS: the design for this species was originally meant to be used for the Lizard Herders.

INSECTOPHAGI: reptiles and arthropods are among my favourite animals, and thus I really enjoyed creating the plate-like jaw articulations on this post-human species.

SPACERS: I referenced bat skeletons when creating the long, spindly limbs of these post-humans.

RUIN HAUNTERS: my aim with these was to create a brutish, arrogant species but without them looking like orcs, trolls or other fantasy monsters. They are the closest *All Tomorrows* comes to a villainous species.

EXTINCT SWIMMER: extensive research into turtle, seal and Late Cretaceous elasmosaur skeletons went into this meticulous painting.

SNAKE PEOPLE: the overall look of the costume the creature is wearing was inspired by director Tim Burton's films.

KILLER FOLK: designing and rendering the character's split-digited hand took longer than the rest of the painting itself.

TOOL BREEDERS: the inspiration for living tools and technology based on animal breeding came from Harry Harrison's 'West of Eden' series of books.

SAUROSAPIENTS: a great challenge in creating this species was referencing archosaurs and other prehistoric reptiles without making them too similar to dinosaurs.

MODULAR PEOPLE: much like the Temptors, this design was pure improvisation.

PTEROSAPIENS: this is my favourite illustration in the entire book. A nice by-product of this setting was the design of the towers with all the irregularly spaced doorways.

ASYMMETRIC PEOPLE: when designing this nightmarish race, I adhered closely to the body-plan I established when creating their Lopsider ancestors. Setting limits actually makes for more creative and realistic creature design.

SYMBIOTES: once again, I enjoyed designing the architecture in the background as much as the creature itself.

SAIL PEOPLE: I really enjoyed subverting expectations with this species. You might naturally expect that their Finger Fisher ancestors to evolve into a mantis-like creature, or a crocodile-like swimmer. I went for a completely different, outlandish design instead.

SATYRIACS: the lead singer here was inspired by David Bowie – still one of my favourite artists.

BUG FACERS: it took me many attempts to get the right balance of uncanny and relatable, of animal and human, attributes for this post-human species. Its eyes are copied from giant legless lizards I used to keep as pets.

SUBJECTS: the best way to obtain wildly creative results in art goes through establishing certain limiting factors. Once I had the Bug Facer anatomy fixed, it was very easy to spin off the zany and contorted forms of the Subjects.

ASTEROMORPHS: the Asteromorphs' big eyes and bulging heads were my hat-tip to alien designs in mid-century American pulp magazines.

GRAVITAL: for these I wanted an instantly recognisable form, stark like a death-mask. The light in the character's central eye is actually the Photoshopped picture of a candle photographed from above.

ASTEROMORPH GODS: I loved the flaring heads and finger-limbs of these majestic beings. This was another completely improvised design.

NEW MACHINES: the tangled limbs and tentacles of the creature that appears in this illustra-tion were inspired by the work of German zoologist and naturalist Haeckel (1834–1919).

AMPHICEPHALUS: easily the zaniest design in this book, the Amphicephalus was actually based on one of my earliest childhood drawings of a 'snake-eat-snake alien' with multiple heads. I wanted to honour my younger self by reinterpreting this creation.

THE AUTHOR: another work of pure improvisation without overreaching concerns. Is the author post-human, Qu or something else entirely? I'll leave that question unanswered . . .

Sketches

Ideas need to evolve, just like organisms! Here are sketches, ranging from basic doodles to full-on pre-render illustrations, showing you the evolution of various *All Tomorrows* creatures, and glimpses of what might have been.

Sketch of a tiny, fruit-eating post-human – one of the many rejected concepts for All Tomorrows.

Another rejected concept sketch, for a race of tiny, reed-dwelling 'stick people'.

Skulls of various post-human species with specialised dentition.

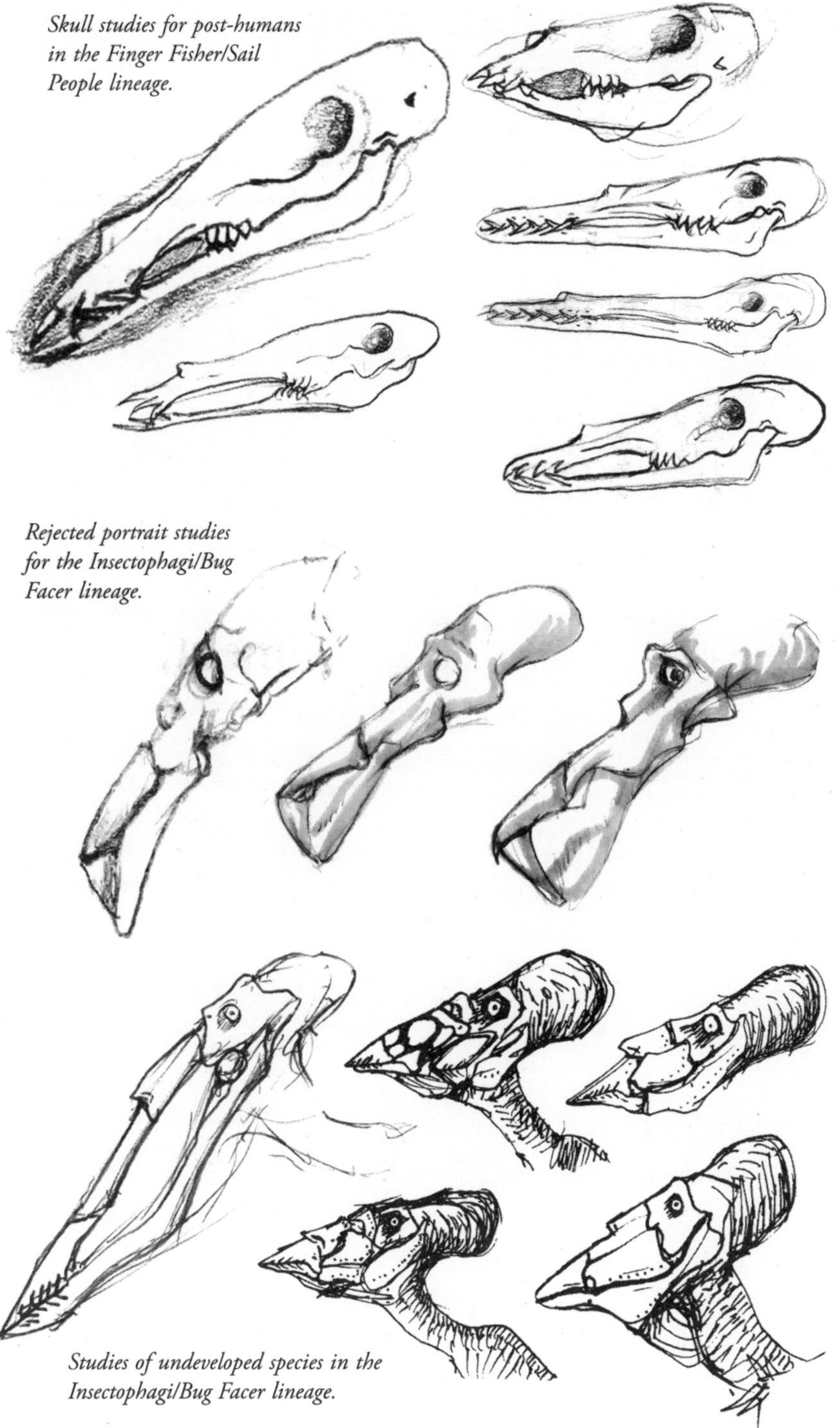

Skull studies for post-humans in the Finger Fisher/Sail People lineage.

Rejected portrait studies for the Insectophagi/Bug Facer lineage.

Studies of undeveloped species in the Insectophagi/Bug Facer lineage.

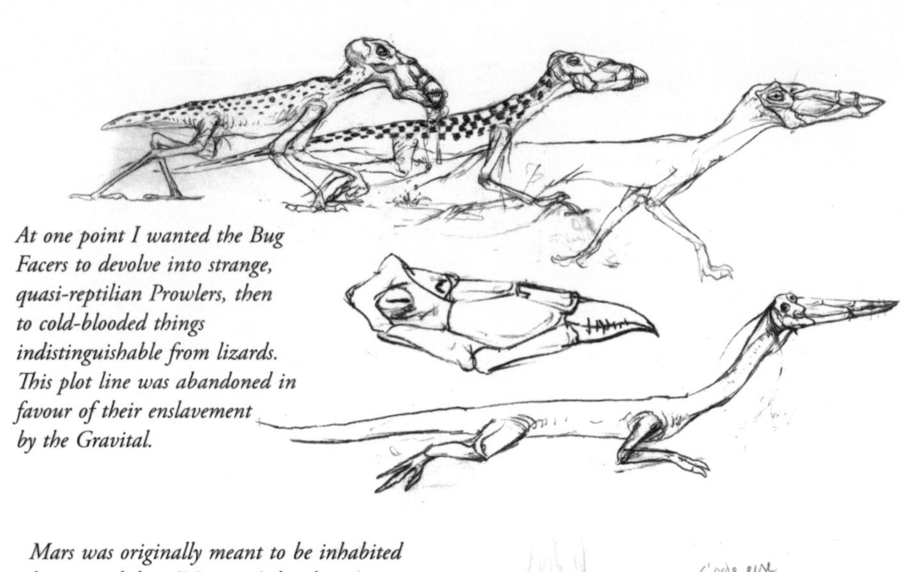

At one point I wanted the Bug Facers to devolve into strange, quasi-reptilian Prowlers, then to cold-blooded things indistinguishable from lizards. This plot line was abandoned in favour of their enslavement by the Gravital.

Mars was originally meant to be inhabited by eerie, gliding 'Martians' that humanity would drive extinct during their colonisation of that planet – genocide as a symbolic 'loss of innocence' as humanity expanded in the solar system.

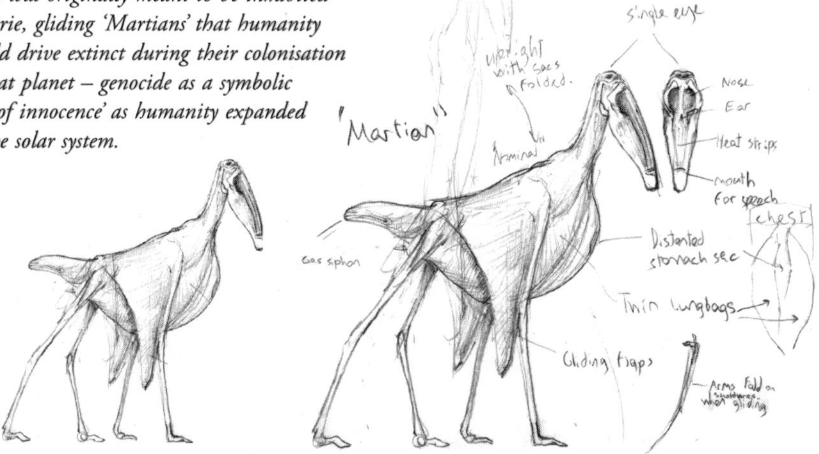

Studies for the Bone Crusher species – at one point I wanted them to have a lanky, quadrupedal body structure.

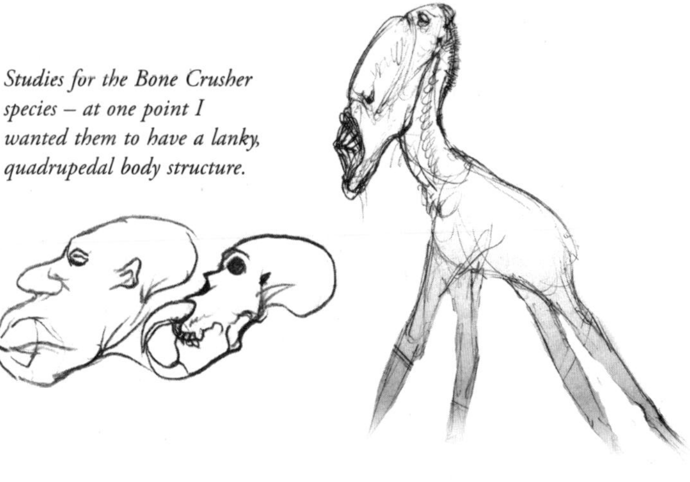

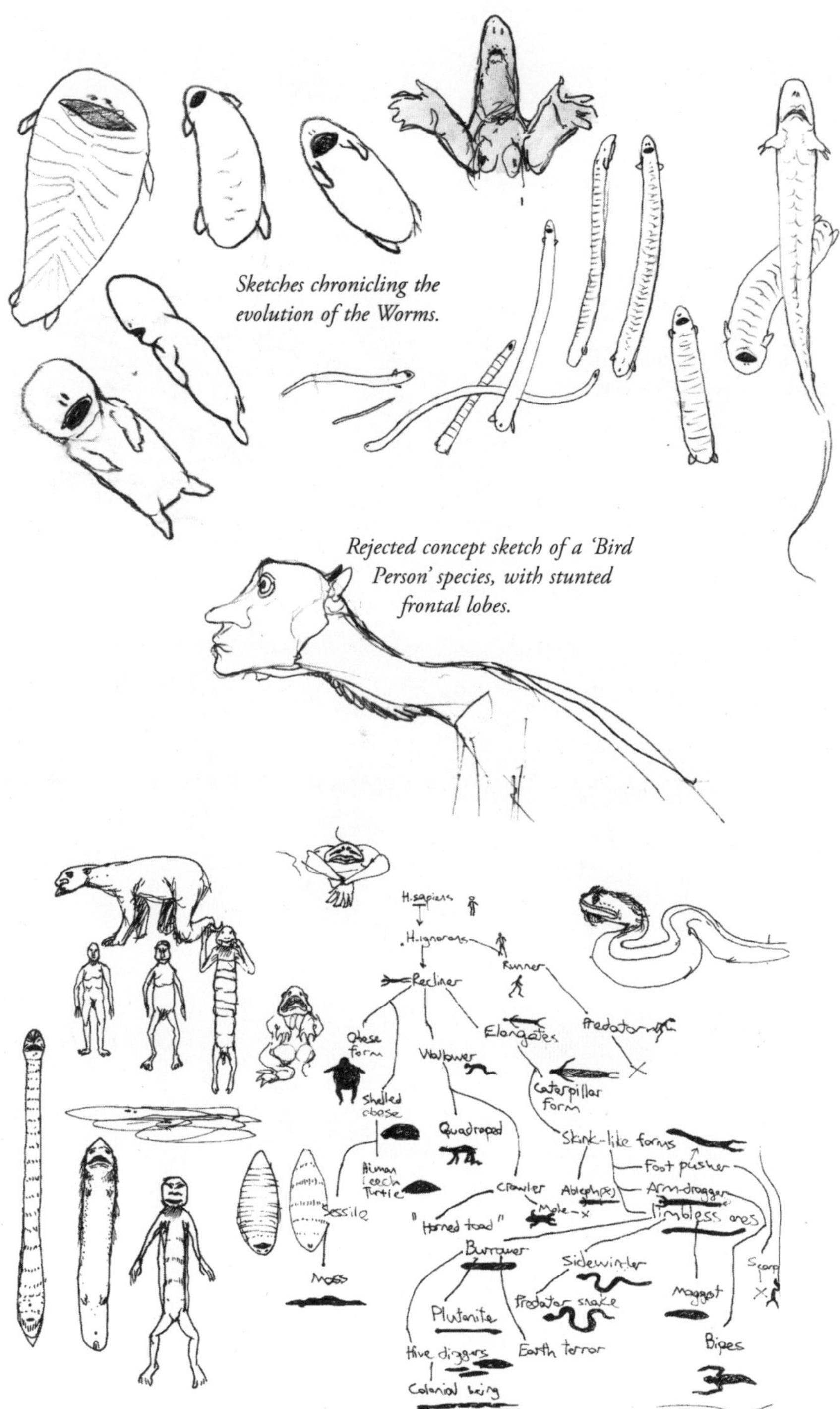

Sketches chronicling the evolution of the Worms.

Rejected concept sketch of a 'Bird Person' species, with stunted frontal lobes.

At one point I imagined a very extensive family tree for the world of the Worms, where humanity would evolve into numerous snake, mole and skink-like forms.

Studies of strange bird/dinosaur creatures for the world where Panderavis *was discovered.*

Ultimately, only Panderavis *was fully illustrated; these other concepts were rejected.*

Sketch of a sessile, 'Ultimate Post-human' species that was meant to persist after humanity's disappearance into another realm of existence. In the end, I did not use this concept.

Sketch of the monstrous 'killer chicken' species that drove the Striders extinct.

Early sketch for the Striders.

Sketches for the Predators/Killer Folk.

Sketch for the Sleepers – a rejected species of lazy, sloth-like post-humans.

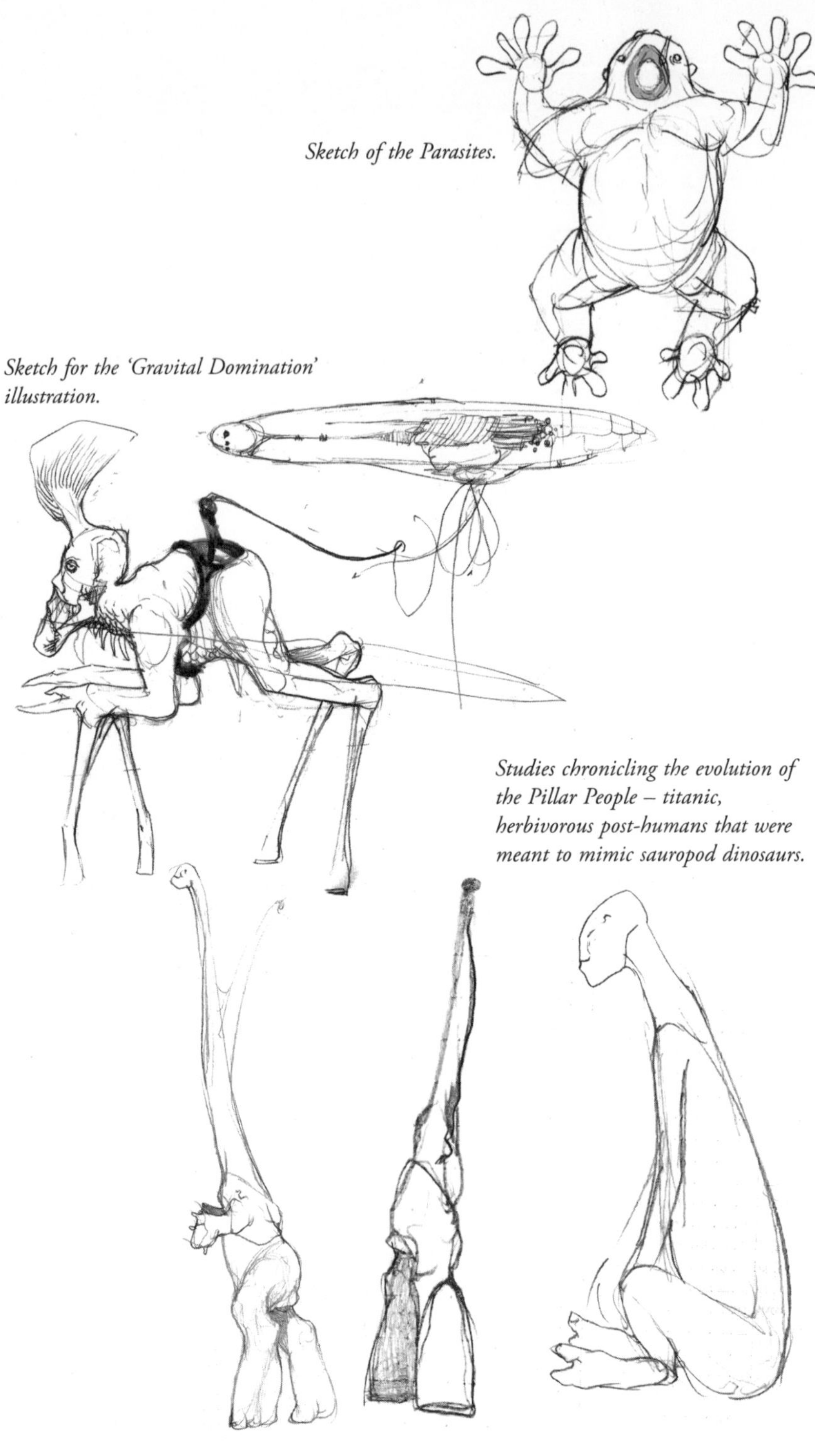

Sketch of the Parasites.

Sketch for the 'Gravital Domination' illustration.

Studies chronicling the evolution of the Pillar People – titanic, herbivorous post-humans that were meant to mimic sauropod dinosaurs.

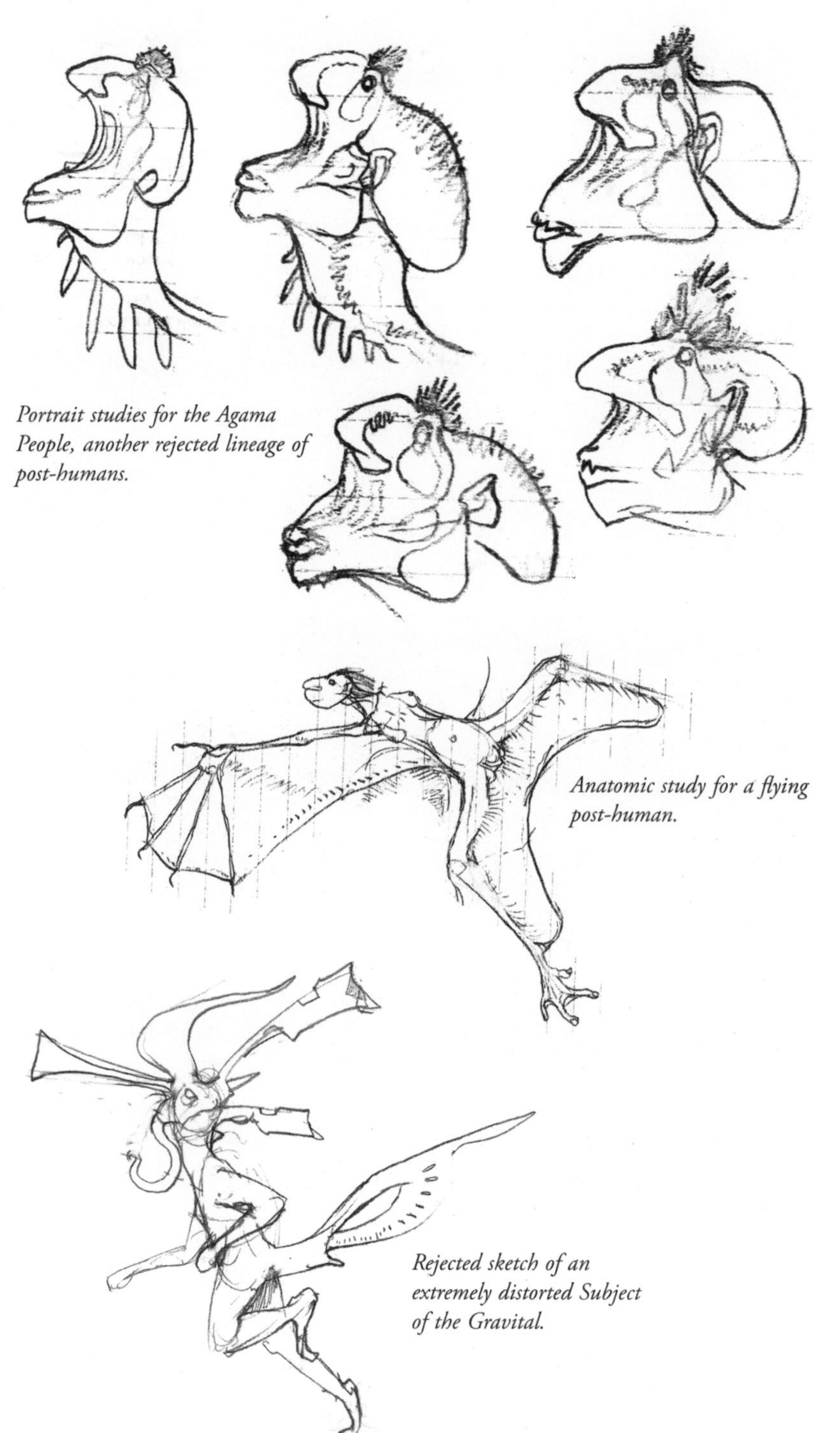

Portrait studies for the Agama People, another rejected lineage of post-humans.

Anatomic study for a flying post-human.

Rejected sketch of an extremely distorted Subject of the Gravital.

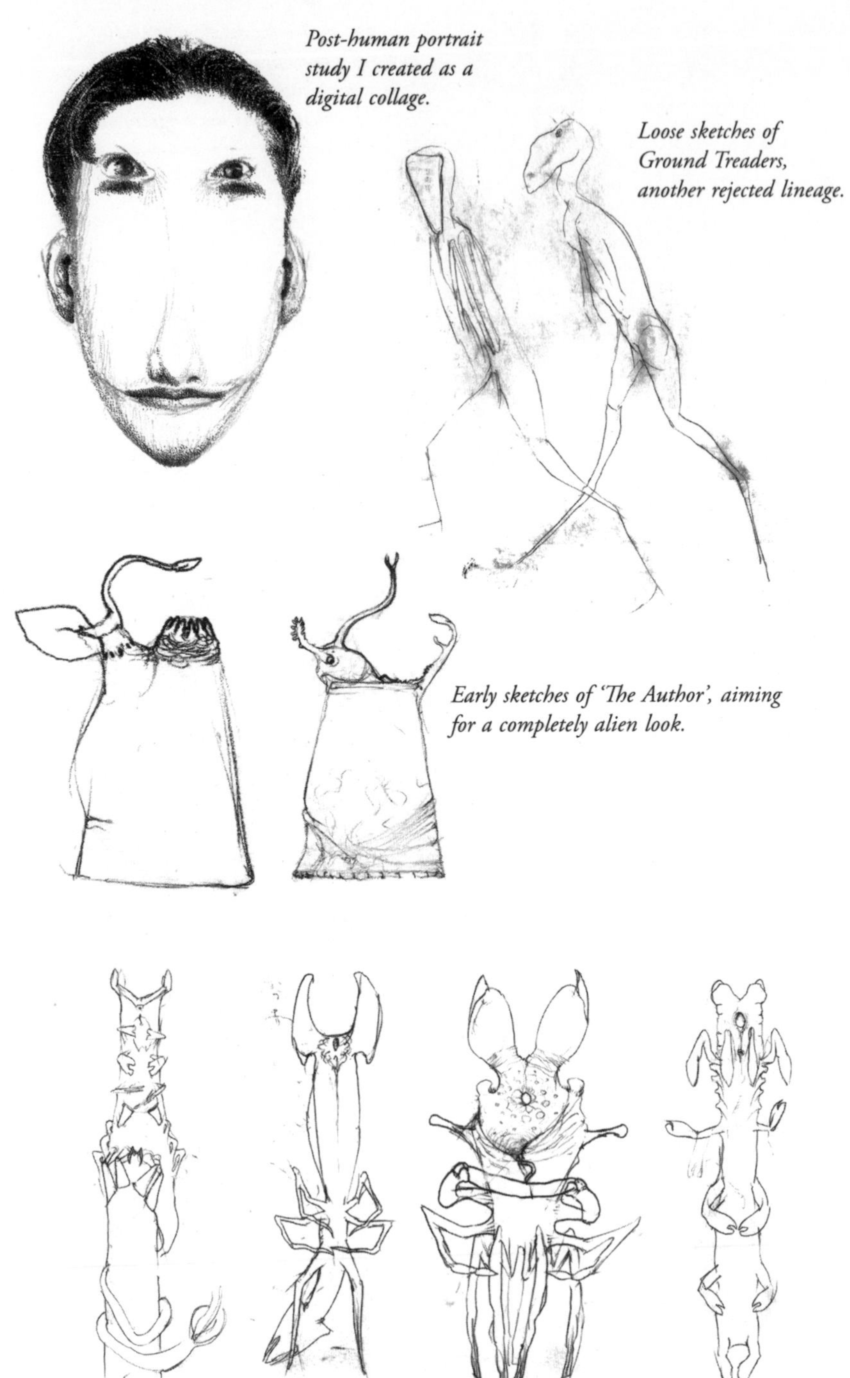

Post-human portrait study I created as a digital collage.

Loose sketches of Ground Treaders, another rejected lineage.

Early sketches of 'The Author', aiming for a completely alien look.

Further developed concept sketches for the 'Author' character.

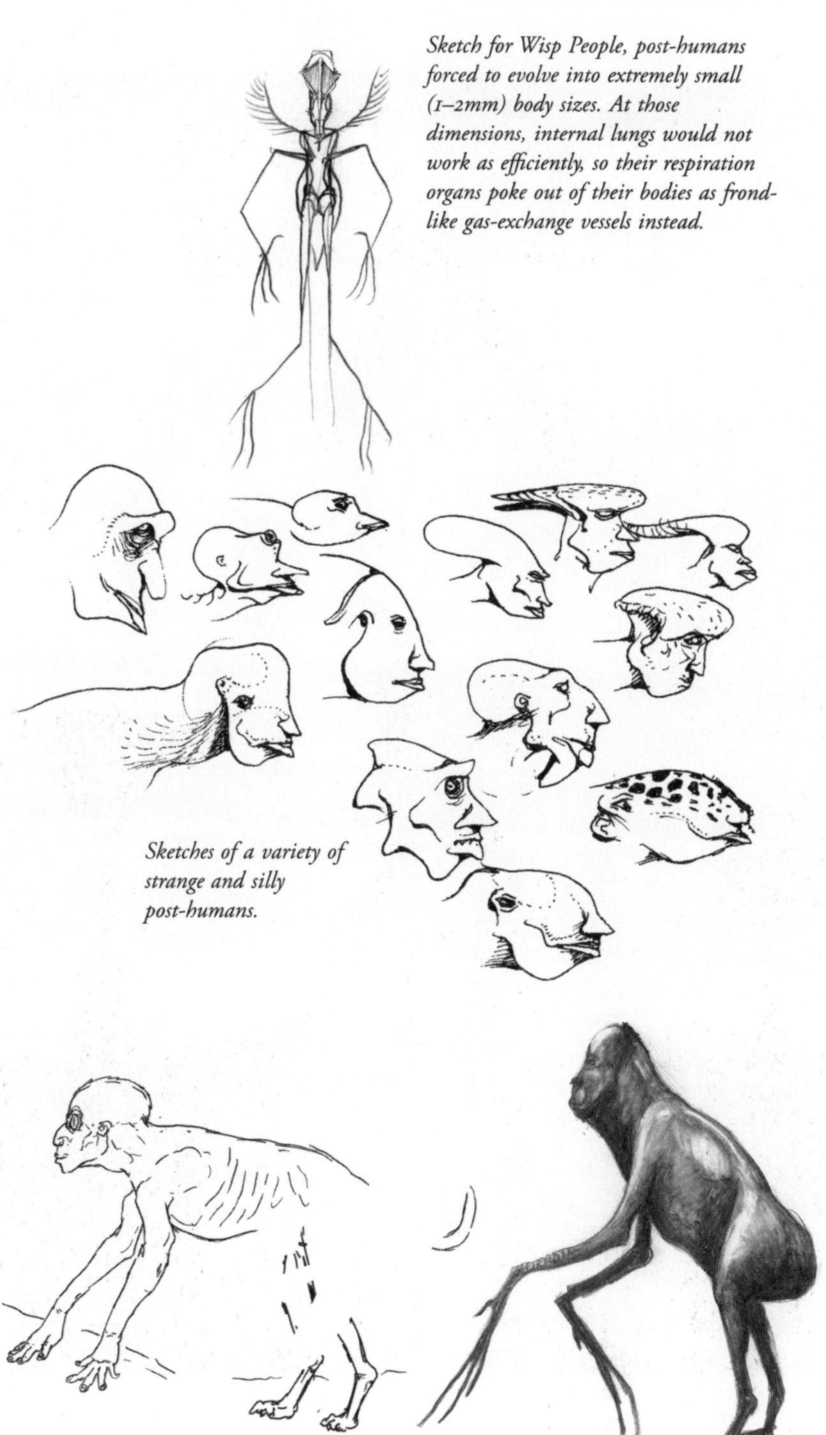

Sketch for Wisp People, post-humans forced to evolve into extremely small (1–2mm) body sizes. At those dimensions, internal lungs would not work as efficiently, so their respiration organs poke out of their bodies as frond-like gas-exchange vessels instead.

Sketches of a variety of strange and silly post-humans.

Two more rejected post-human concepts.

A 'Wind-Eater' post-human sophont from a deleted story arc.

The Making of *All Tomorrows*

Since I first released *All Tomorrows* online in 2006, 'speculative evolution' (the art of imagining plausible organisms in fictional timelines and circumstances) has gained an entire new generation of fans. Speculative evolution can be about aliens, or it can focus on scenarios based on pre-existing organisms, such as the future evolution of human beings, an alternate world where dinosaurs had survived, a planet populated entirely by canaries and guppy fish, and so on.

Speculative evolution artists are unique in being able to harness the flames of art and science together. At the time of this book's publication, the internet and social media are thriving with such imagined ecosystems and art projects, each showcasing the knowledge and artistic skills of its creator.

I am really happy that *All Tomorrows* has its own contribution to the growth of this new, exciting non-narrative art form. Almost daily, I get fan questions about what inspired me, and since you have invested in this present volume it would be only fair to reflect on what inspired and motivated me as I wrote and illustrated *All Tomorrows* in the early 2000s.

No author is an island, not even if you are writing science fiction or fantasy. You simply cannot form ideas in a vacuum. Therefore, a basic background in evolution and biology, alongside a basic knowledge of anatomical drawing, would be ideal for any budding speculative-evolution enthusiast.

Despite my interest in nature, art was my primary inspiration, especially surreal and grotesque art. I was not interested in weirdness for weirdness's sake, but when alien forms were combined with coherent back stories and world-building, a very particular area was tickled in my brain.

Back in those days, it was difficult to find such niche material. The internet was still in its infancy, and actual books were hard to access. I was very lucky to have a copy of *The Alien Life of Wayne Barlowe*, and it inspired me immensely. I remember carrying it around everywhere I went, even to family dinners, gatherings with friends and other occasions where I did not expect to have time to read it.

As the saying goes, books beget more books, and within the pages of Wayne Barlowe's *Alien Life* I found references to a book 'which would have dealt, in quasi-scientific manner, with the possible evolution of Mankind in the distant future'. I searched around the internet – this was still the era of dial-up connections and modems – and found Dougal Dixon's *Man After Man: An Anthropology of the Future*. I was hooked.

A lot of influences came from those books, and more; Olaf Stapledon's *Star Maker* and *Last and First Men*, Robert Silverberg's *Son of Man*, Robert Charles Wilson's *Darwinia* and Larry Niven's 'Ringworld' series, with its wild cast of post-humans, greatly inspired *All Tomorrows*. Even the *Star Wars* universe was an inspiration, not for its space battles and grandiose themes of good versus evil, but for the insane variety of strange, scary or just plain goofy characters that haunted the background of its cantinas, palaces and space ports. The book first began as a portfolio of weird, zany post-human drawings, and the story around them developed later on.

At this point, I must also tell a little about my own life, and the events I experienced while writing this book. Drawing and writing *All Tomorrows* took place between roughly 2001 and 2006. In that time, I went from seventeen to twenty-two years old. In retrospect, it is easy to see the psychological imprint of maturing in the themes of humans evolving and then mutating into alien forms. I drew strange post-humans as my body grew, my mind warped and my attraction to others began. Adolescence is hard-baked into *All Tomorrows*.

Another theme, that of death, extinction, and irretrievable loss, also impacted my life at that time. I lost a loved grandparent in the Izmit Earthquake of 1999, and another passed away two years later. More deaths and loss followed. Throughout it all, I realised that life had a way of going on, and this in turn became an early inoculation against fear. Looking back, I can see how these events were formative in the interwoven themes of hope and loss in *All Tomorrows*.

Other, minor details also had roles to play. My joy at finding sea cucumbers and brittle stars in rock pools inspired the lifestyle of the Finger Fishers; insects and reptiles I found during days of skipping school, wandering out to a meadow and turning over stones, led to the Insectophagi species and others. Memories of a childhood spent exploring abandoned buildings, not to mention Byzantine, Lycian and Seljukid ruins during vacations across Turkey translated directly into the sentiment of the Ruin Haunters.

Illustrating the Finger Fisher species for *All Tomorrows* on a boat trip across the Eastern Aegean with my family. I am nineteen years old in this photograph (please excuse my goatee!). The idea for the Finger Fishers came to me naturally after spending days exploring the splash zone on the shores seen in the background, prying in between rocks to find all manner of sea creatures.

Visually, too, I scavenged to create textures for images in the book. I had a primitive digital camera and took pictures of every interesting surface I came across. My mother's kitchen pans became the background for the Asteromorphs, bubbles in a glass of beer became the 'galactic explosion' in the background as the Gravital were defeated, and my own skin provided the texture for many of the creatures in this book.

The point I am making is this: your personal experiences contribute to the ingenuity and uniqueness of a fictional project almost as much as, if not more than, your repository of topical knowledge. It is the subconscious layer beneath the visible surface of creatures, events and storylines. Balancing it is indeed a tricky task: too much 'personal experience' and a story will reek of conceit. Too little, and the final effort will be 'saltless', bland.

Getting the right mix is a lifelong task. My advice is: read a lot, draw a lot. Never stop working and try to include something from your heart in your work. Don't aim to make a book from the get-go; instead, hone your skills and find out what you want to focus on. And most of all: have fun! I hope reading this short behind-the-scenes account of the making of *All Tomorrows* helps and inspires your own creative efforts.

Selfie with a wild-caught Pallas's glass lizard, *Pseudopus apodus* – the direct inspiration for the Snake People in *All Tomorrows*. I also used its eyes as the eyes of th Bug Facer portrait.

If you ever want to correspond about writing and illustrating speculative evolution, my email address at the time of publication is: c.m.kosemen@gmail.com Depending on my time, I try to respond to every email and letter.